His Captive Lover

Elizabeth Lennox

CONTENTS

Chapter 1

Autumn looked at the list, her eyes casually skimming down the cases. When her eyes caught one name in particular, she looked again, shocked and not believing her eyes. When she looked one more time, she gasped, still not sure she believed that this name was on this particular list. Sure enough, the name hadn't changed when she refocused.

Panic filled her and she looked around, wondering what she could do. This couldn't be happening! Of all the names that might have popped up on the court's docket roster, this one was the only one that Autumn never would have expected.

"Ash!" she whispered, suddenly knowing exactly what she needed to do.

Running down the stairs then through the long hallway, she burst into the office on the left corner. The large, intimidating man sitting behind the steel and glass desk seemed to be the day's super hero, at least when it came to this impossible situation. "Help!" she cried out as she burst into his office, not even bothering to knock as she normally would.

Ash looked up, his black eyebrows rising above his strange, blue eyes. "What's wrong?" he asked of the normally ultra-professional, uber-polite-except-when-a-certain-brother-was-around office manager. She rushed into his office, her eyes wide with an emotion that didn't make sense on her beautiful features. Ash watched as she hurried around his desk, remaining calm despite Autumn's panic.

"Please, you have to get her out of there!" she rushed over to his desk and slapped the list down in front of him then immediately turned to figure out what he might need to solve this horrible problem. She hurried behind his desk and grabbed the suit jacket that had been draped across the back of his chair, grabbing his hand and sticking it into the sleeve even while he read the paper she'd slapped in front of him seconds ago.

Ash looked down at the paper, still remaining calm even while he allowed her to help him into his jacket. "This is a list of the people being arraigned this morning." He transferred the paper to his other hand, still reading. With practiced coordination, Autumn grabbed the other hand to stuff it into the sleeve, then pushed the jacket onto his enormous shoulders.

Autumn didn't even bother to look at the paper again, too frantic to get the impossibly large man moving. "Correct. The person you're going to save is the third name down on that list." She grabbed his briefcase and haphazardly stuffed some papers into it, then looked around to see if there was anything else he might need.

Ash looked at the name. "Mia Paulson?"

"Yes! You have to go help her!" She ordered him and shoved his leather chair out of the way while she put her hands up on his shoulders, pushing his enormous body around his desk and out the door. She'd never been so bold before, but she didn't have time to be nice. This was an emergency.

Ash stopped moving and turned around to look down into Autumn's worried, chocolate eyes. "Looks like she's being arraigned for first degree murder."

Autumn looked up at the man who was the only one who could save her friend. Unfortunately, she had to take a precious moment to explain because Ash was too large and too muscular to move when he didn't want to. "She's my best friend and I guarantee that she's innocent. But more importantly, she's probably trying to do this all on her own because she naively believes in the justice system and probably thinks her claim of innocence will get her out of this mess." Autumn was already shaking her head and waving her hands in the air. "There's no way Mia could have killed anyone. She composts all of her plants. She scoots bugs out of her house instead of stomping on them like a normal person. When we're walking down the sidewalk, she'll actually stop and help earthworms get across so they don't dehydrate in the sunshine and die. So killing a human being is completely outside the realm of possibility. Unfortunately, you're her only hope and you've got to do something!" she explained, her voice rising towards the end as her patience in explaining things to Ash wore thin. There wasn't time to talk. The court would be in session in just a few minutes so Ash had to hurry and get over to the courthouse now!

Ash couldn't help it. The image of Autumn with her three inch heels and her pencil skirts, her long, dark hair looking so prim and proper walking with someone who helped earthworms and bugs was just amusing and he let out a deep chuckle. "So she's a saint. But even saints have a breaking point and, when provoked, can kill someone if rage or passion takes over."

"First of all, that wouldn't be first degree murder, would it? Besides, you're thinking of normal people like me when I'm talking to your obnoxious brother,

Xander. Not Mia! We've known each other since elementary school," she said, gathering up his planner and extra pens, stuffing everything into his case in a haphazard manner. She walked behind him again, trying to shove him out of the office which was impossible unless Ash Thorpe was willing to be pushed. He was simply too big.

Thankfully, he allowed himself to be moved along, then pushed out the door. "You have to hurry. She's being arraigned any minute now and she's probably terrified. She definitely doesn't understand the process because she's a school teacher. The woman doesn't even have a parking ticket to her name so she has no clue how harsh the justice system can be. She needs you and you have to hurry!"

Ash grabbed another file on the way out, shaking his head at the odd situation. "If she's being charged with murder, where was she at the time of the crime? What is the evidence the police have on her? What's the motive?" he asked.

"I don't know!" she snapped, pushing him from behind now, picturing her friend's worried face as she sat in a jail cell with all the other criminals who might hurt her because Mia was such a nice, innocent woman who believed in human kindness. "Stop asking questions and move faster!" she ordered him, completely forgetting that she was the office manager while Ash Thorpe was one of the partners of the illustrious Thorpe Group legal team that consisted of four brilliant brothers who all worked in different areas of the law. Not to mention Ash Thorpe was also the best criminal attorney in the country. People hired Ash from all over the United States to get him to defend them.

"Don't you need your coat?" he asked, looking down at her silk blouse. He rarely saw Autumn without her matching suit jacket. She might take it off in her office, but she slipped it on if she had any reason to step out of her area. They were out in the cool October morning with a definite bite to the air.

She shook her head, barely even acknowledging his question in her urgency to get him out the door. "Not now." She led him over to her small car with a combination of forceful nudges, pulls and racing ahead of him to challenge him to keep up with her. When they finally arrived at her car, she opened the passenger seat and practically pushed him in, ignoring the humor of seeing his large, muscular frame sitting inside her tiny vehicle. At his questioning look, she said, "I'll drive. You'll be too slow. We might not make it in time."

He looked at her askance even as he whipped his foot out of the way before she slammed the door on it. "I'm too slow?" he asked with astonishment, but only the dust inside her car heard him since she was almost running around to the driver's side. He chuckled slightly as he shook his head. No one had ever accused him of being slow. He stepped out of the car and she froze, her wide, chocolate eyes begging him to get back into the car.

3

"Autumn, what's going on here? I'm never slow and court is almost in session."

She was becoming frustrated with his delays and questions. "Stop messing around! Mia needs your help! You're the one who always thinks that justice has to be done and here you are just standing here mocking me." She paused a moment, tears threatening her eyes. "Please, Ash. You're really the only one I would trust. She's my best friend and I know she's terrified right now and probably very confused."

Ash took pity on her and turned serious. Looking at her from across the roof of her car, he smiled reassuringly. Or as soothingly as he could without any knowledge of the situation. "Don't worry, Autumn. I'll help your friend. Judge Rooney is on the bench today. If your friend is third on the docket, we still have plenty of time to meet up with her. You can drive and on the way, I'll call some of my sources and find out what's going on, get the evidence against her and find out who is prosecuting. Okay?" he asked with that famous Ash Thorpe confidence.

She smiled, instantly relieved that he was finally on board with the issue. "Thank you!" she replied. But a moment later, she pointed for him to get back into the car and, even in her rush, gracefully slid in behind the wheel.

She ignored Ash as he made some phone calls, only hearing his end of the conversation as she focused on the early morning traffic. Thankfully, The Thorpe Group's offices were close to the courthouse but downtown Chicago traffic was still obnoxiously difficult.

Fifteen minutes later, Autumn swallowed painfully as she pulled into the courthouse parking lot. The expression on Ash's face scared her more than anything. "What's wrong?" she asked, parking in one of the empty spaces near the courthouse.

"Pretty much everything," Ash said and opened the car door. All signs of humor and resistance were gone now, replaced by that cold, logical determination that had made him so famous in previous trials. The man certainly loved his job, but when he grasped onto a situation, he was like a pit bull, not stopping for anything until he'd succeeded. "Come on. We have our work cut out for us." With that, he strode up the steps of the courthouse and worked his way through security. Once he was clear, he and Autumn rushed through the doors of the courtroom.

Right before he entered, he touched Autumn's arm to stop her. Looking down into her worried eyes he said, "Autumn, you need to let me do my job. I know this is your friend, but I'm going to treat her just as I would any other client. I have to in order to get her out of there."

Autumn swallowed, painfully aware that Mia was still waiting. She had no idea what Ash was telling her, but she nodded in agreement. When he started to turn back to enter the courtroom, she stopped him with a hand on his arm. When he was once again looking down at her, she explained the harsh truth to him. "She can't pay," Autumn said softly. "I'll pay your fees. Please, just help her."

Ash sighed, the issue becoming more complicated. Autumn might look professional and tough and she fought his older brother tooth and nail on anything she considered an important issue, not afraid to stand up for what she believed in. But Ash had worked with this woman for several years now. He knew that, deep down inside, Autumn was a soft, sweet, kind person which made her vulnerable to the harshness of life. "And what if she's guilty?" he asked carefully, needing her to face the possibility.

Autumn shook her head. "No. She isn't. You'll see. Wait until you meet her before you make a judgment. You'll know as soon as you look into her eyes. She's just a thoughtful, gentle person who teaches kids and loves her job and gardens as a hobby. She doesn't do anything wrong except stand up for the little guy."

Ash looked at her for a long moment. This would be a complicated case and if it weren't for Autumn's personal involvement, Ash wouldn't even take it. It seemed like an open and shut case from what his police source said. The only issue in their favor is that the police hadn't found the body of the victim yet.

He sighed, turning to fully face her so he could ensure that she understood how bad this looked for her friend. "Autumn, there's an eyewitness that said Mia Paulson and the victim were in a fight the day the victim went missing. The man your friend is accused of killing? It's her ex-fiancé. Your friend apparently was jilted for another woman." He shook his head and sighed. "Her fingerprints are even on a piece of evidence that has the victim's blood on it. It's an old baseball trophy with one of those heavy bottoms and the police think it is the murder weapon. It's a pretty tight case for the prosecution. If I were on the jury, I'd vote to convict her without even hearing the prosecution's arguments."

Autumn's eyes hardened as she listened to Ash's recitation of all he'd learned on the drive over here. And it just made her angrier. "If that bastard did this, you make him pay, Ash! Mia wasn't dumped. She broke up with him. Not only did she get rid of him, but their breakup was a while ago. Mia isn't mean or petty but she'd discovered some irritating things about her ex-fiancé and broke up with him. He wouldn't accept the breakup though. He stalked her and drove her nuts. Please, hurry and you'll see!" she begged.

Ash shook his head, wondering why he was even entering into the courtroom under these circumstances. "Autumn, you have to..."

She held up her hand to stop him. "If the evidence is that bad against her, then she needs your talents all the more. Please," she begged once again, "you're her only hope. You're the only one I know of that could help her get out of this mess."

Ash sighed and nodded his head. "Just don't get your hopes up, okay?"

Autumn's bright smile struck him and he wondered why his older brother Xander didn't do something about his feelings for this woman. Autumn was extremely intelligent, stunningly beautiful and obviously in love with Xander. In Ash's mind, the two made a perfect couple. And if the sparks flying around the office between the two combatants lately were any indication, there was either going to be a wedding to attend, or a funeral. Although he wasn't sure which.

"Let's do this," he said and stepped through the doors. Normally, he would spend time with his clients before their arraignment, find out any extenuating circumstances and get control of the courtroom. But because his new "client" was about to be announced any moment, he didn't have time for that today.

"People versus Mia Paulson, murder in the first degree," the court clerk at the front of the courtroom announced with his loud, bellowing voice.

As always, the courtroom was chaotic and filled with people milling about, attorneys speaking with their clients, family members moving around and talking amongst themselves, police officers conferring with district attorneys as well as the prosecuting and defense attorneys calling out their cases to the judge. It wasn't like the old fashioned courtrooms one saw on television but an ultra-modern room where the back was darker than the front and the judge sat on his throne-like chair in front of all the chaos, looking bored and irritated by the bother.

Into this mix stepped Ash while Autumn sat down in one of the rows, feeling better now that Ash was on board and taking charge. She scanned the room and tried to smile reassuringly as the police officer brought Mia forward.

Mia stepped up to the defense table, her eyes wide with fear and her whole body trembling. She couldn't believe this was actually happening. How had her life gotten so out of control?

She was wearing jeans and a tee-shirt instead of a professional looking suit. Since the police had banged on her door in the early hours of the morning, she didn't have any make-up on, her hair was a mess and she was terrified out of her mind. The police had arrived with a warrant for her arrest about four o'clock in the morning, waking her up out of a sound sleep and tossing questions and a piece of paper at her moments before they started rummaging around in her house. She'd answered the door in her robe, pushing her brown curls out of her eyes and trying very hard to focus. And now she stood in front of a busy courtroom, her mind frantically trying to figure out what was happening.

"Do you have counsel?" the judge barked out over the noise of the audience.

Mia looked around, finally figuring out that the judge was talking to her. A lawyer? Was this really happening to her? "Umm…" she started to say but she didn't have a chance to answer the judge. She was about to open her mouth but was stopped by someone behind her.

"Ash Thorpe here to represent Ms. Paulson, Your Honor," a deep, commanding voice said.

Mia looked around, her grey eyes scanning the crowd. A super tall man was stepping out of the crowd and her eyes widened in shock. She looked up into his blue eyes, wondering why he was here, who he was and why he was coming forward. A man this gorgeous shouldn't be in a courtroom. And he definitely shouldn't be standing next to her. But then, she shouldn't be here either! She should be rushing out of her little cottage home, dropping her keys onto the wooden steps and grumbling as she bent down to pick them up again as she raced down the stairs so she could get to school before her kids started arriving. She should be worrying about spilling her coffee on her suit as she fought the traffic into the city.

Instead, because of some weird, unexplainable twist of life, she was standing here, defending herself against a murder charge. Surely this was some sort of nightmare and she'd wake up in a moment. The sky would be lightening on the horizon and she'd figure out that she needed to wear a lighter suit instead of a wool one because it was going to be a hot, fall day instead of those delicious, cool ones that made her feel more motivated.

No, this horrible moment wasn't happening to her.

"How does your defendant plead?" the judge demanded over the din.

"Not guilty, Your Honor," the gorgeous man stated confidently. He stood right next to her, but didn't even bother to consult her on any of the issues. "We request that the defendant be released on her own recognizance," the crazy-tall man was saying.

The prosecutor spoke up and Mia's eyes swung over in that direction, completely confused about what was being said. Was this about her or another case? "The defendant is accused of murdering her ex-fiancé out of jealousy. The people request that the defendant be remanded until trial."

Tall-Gorgeous-Dude shook his head, his eyes glaring at the prosecutor. "Ms. Paulson doesn't have even a parking ticket to her name," the tall, muscular man called back, his voice confident and deep, sexy and Mia couldn't believe that she was thinking something like that while her entire life was at stake. "She hasn't been engaged to the supposed victim in four months, nor does the prosecution even have the body of which Ms. Paulson might have murdered."

The judge swung his eyes back to the prosecutor with irritation, stunned that the prosecutor would bring a murder charge without a body. "Is that true?" he asked.

The prosecutor shook his head, "The victim has been missing for more than a week. His blood was found on the murder weapon with Ms. Paulson's fingerprints."

The judge shook his head. "If there's no body, it sounds like you can't even prove that there's a murder. The man might have just left and gone to an island somewhere," the judge grumbled, obviously wishing he could do the same thing.

Tall-Gorgeous-Dude stepped in at that moment. "Since there's no body and the prosecution can't prove that there's even been a murder, I request that the charges against my client be dropped, Your Honor." Mia's eyes swung from the tall man beside her to the judge, praying with hope that the man in the black robes would agree with this stranger.

The prosecutor spoke up quickly. "The current fiancée to the victim swears that the victim wouldn't disappear. He's a principal at the local high school with enormous responsibilities. And there was a great deal of blood in the victim's house. Too much blood for there not to be foul play. We currently have investigators at Ms. Paulson's house digging up her back yard, searching for the body. We are confident that we will find it by mid-morning."

The judge considered the opposing arguments and came to a speedy conclusion. "Since there's no body, I won't hold the defendant. But the case can continue to trial and I'll let the presiding judge hear whether there's enough evidence to move forward. Defendant is released on her own recognizance, but must surrender her passport to the court until trial." The gavel banged down and another voice was calling out the next case.

Mia felt her arm grasped in a firm, demanding grip and she was pulled out of the courtroom. She still wasn't sure what was going on, but she felt the tall man's body next to hers, felt the trembling start up but for a completely different reason this time.

And then she saw Autumn and the tears burst out of her. "You're here!" Mia exclaimed and rushed forward, grabbing her friend around her shoulders and hugging her with all her strength. "I can't believe this is happening!" she sobbed out. Mia was shorter than Autumn, but only because of her best friend's love of spike heels.

Autumn held Mia in her arms and mouthed the word, "Thank you," to Ash who was still standing behind the slender woman.

Ash looked down at the two women hugging each other. The one he'd just been defending was sobbing and he felt only somewhat guilty to notice that the woman looked exceptionally fine in her tight jeans that hugged her bottom so perfectly. He stood there waiting, wanting to see if the woman looked as good from the front as she did from the back. She had softly curling brown hair that ended at her shoulders and his fingers actually ached to touch one of those curls. She was too slender, he thought. While she hugged Autumn, her shirt pulled against her back and he could see her ribs through the thin material. She needed to gain a good ten pounds and he wondered if she'd lost weight because of her recent breakup. He knew women generally either stopped eating when emotionally distraught, or they ate everything in sight. At least, that was the stereotype. He actually had no idea if it were true or not, steering clear of women during emotional upheavals. He preferred the happy, fun and sexy type to the drama queen.

Mia pulled back from her friend, her worried eyes looking up at her. "Thank you!" she said with heartfelt sincerity.

Autumn shook her head as she continued to hold Mia close, still not over the horror of watching her friend come into the courtroom from the menacing holding cells. "Why didn't you call me this morning? I only found out about these ridiculous charges about twenty minutes ago and we had to rush over here to help. I practically had to kidnap Ash to get him over here in time."

Ignoring the reference to the name "Ash", suspecting he was the tall, intimidating man standing behind her, Mia sighed and looked down. "I guess I was pretty ashamed. I don't know what's going on, but I can't figure out what happened to Jeff and nor can the police. They found blood on something and now they assume I killed him." She looked frantically at her friend, desperate for Autumn to not think she could have done something like that. "I haven't spoken to him for over a month and that was only to tell him to leave me alone."

Autumn put her arms around her friend and shook her head, silently reassuring her friend. "I told you that guy was a loser."

Mia laughed but it sounded more like a cry. "I know. Everyone told me that but I didn't listen. I'll definitely listen the next time." She looked around at the people milling all over the wide hallway. "Although, I honestly can't imagine being interested in a guy after this. I didn't even know that Jeff was dead until the police were handcuffing me this morning." She put a hand to her mouth, trying to control the emotions that were threatening to overwhelm her.

Autumn smiled and straightened up. "Don't worry. If anyone can get to the bottom of this situation, it will be Ash. He's the best criminal defense attorney in the world."

Mia turned around, ready to thank the man who had gotten her out of that horrible holding cell. But as soon as she turned around, she froze. Looking up at the man while her life was being threatened was one thing. But looking up at him now, she was stunned by both his height and his breadth. It wasn't that the man was fat. Quite the opposite in fact. His stomach was flat and his legs long and apparently muscular. But those shoulders! She'd actually stood next to this behemoth for all that time? Surely not! She would have noticed those shoulders before. He must be about six foot, four inches tall!

And those eyes! They were a clear, amazing blue, but there was a ring of yellow around the iris, causing her to blink as she looked up at him.

"This is Ash Thorpe," Autumn was saying. "Ash, this is your new client, Mia Paulson."

Ash looked down at the woman and gritted his teeth. Mia was not just a pretty woman. She was stunning! Her soft, grey eyes complimented her pale skin. Her lips were pale right now, but he suspected that was only due to the shock she'd just endured. And she was smiling at him! This woman had just been arrested and accused of murder, and she was smiling warmly at him, looking up at him with admiration and joy.

"It is a pleasure to meet you," Mia said, forcing her face to form a smile despite the fact that she wanted to just melt into a pool of humiliation. This man was so sophisticated, so elegant and so amazingly gorgeous and he'd just gotten her out of jail! Here she was in her worn out jeans and a tee-shirt that had definitely seen better days while he stood in front of her wearing a suit that probably cost more than she made in a whole month.

She felt like she might actually be drooling as she took in the suave, sophisticated giant of a man but then her circumstances occurred to her. She was off men as of four o'clock this morning. She'd made that vow while curled up in a jail cell, trying to get the black stuff off from her fingers after being fingerprinted and her mug shot taken. Her mug shot! How humiliating!

All that had occurred this morning was because she'd found one man cute and adorable. Jeff Richardson had been sweet and charming and had the silliest grin but now he was gone, missing, and everyone thought she'd killed him. Of all the things she did not need in her life at this moment, it was a gorgeous man who looked like he knew his way around a bedroom with his eyes closed.

Ash tore his eyes away from the lovely brunette and glared at his office manager. Autumn was smiling up at Ash, then at her friend and back again, trying to gauge their reactions to each other. That look told him that she knew exactly what was going through his mind.

Looking back down at the other woman, he extended his hand and enveloped her tiny one in his hand. He felt her trembling and every instinct inside of him ordered him to pull her into his arms and hold her tight, to reassure her that he would take care of everything. Where this protective instinct had come from, he had no clue. Women were nice and soft and warm and he loved when one was in his bed. But Mia Paulson didn't appear to be that kind of woman. Which was a problem, because not only did he want to hold her close, taste those full lips and discover all the secrets of her slender figure, but he wanted to hold her close and tell her that all this craziness would go away.

But he couldn't guarantee that. This woman might be a murderer. He knew almost nothing about her, about her case or about her past.

So why was he feeling like someone could tip him over with a feather?

Clearing his throat and pulling his eyes away from those soft, grey ones, he straightened up and told himself to not be fooled by a pretty face. "Let's go back to my office," he grumbled. He dropped the woman's hand and pushed his way through the crowd, grabbing onto the lovely Ms. Paulson's arm to make sure she stayed close to him. It wasn't that he thought she would spirit away from him. No, it was more that he needed the physical connection. Strangely, after holding her hand in his, he didn't feel right without that link. He'd touched her hand and now he wanted to touch all of her. He didn't want her out of his sight. Not because he thought she was guilty. Only because he wanted to feast his eyes on her beautiful features for the next....twenty hours or so. Yes, perhaps that would be enough time to get over the impact of those pretty, soft, grey eyes.

Mia scrambled to keep up with the taller man's longer stride but she couldn't seem to break his hold on her arm and she was practically running to keep pace with him. Even Autumn had problems matching his pace as they raced through the marble hallways and her friend was looking at her boss as if he'd just grown a second and third head.

"Ash, wait up!" Autumn called out, trying to slow him down. She couldn't keep up in these shoes and she caught Mia's desperate, confused look as well.

Ash didn't listen. He walked out to Autumn's car and opened the back door, placing the mystery woman in the back. "I'll drive," he said and plucked the keys out of Autumn's fingers.

Thankfully, Autumn didn't argue but got into the passenger seat while he walked around to the other side.

"I have no idea what's gotten into him, Mia," she said while both women watched his long stride as he walked around the engine of the car. "He's usually much more charming."

Mia wanted to reply, but the man she'd just thought of as handsome and delicious, but now knew was arrogant and a big, huge jerk, was now getting into the driver's seat and pushing back the seat to accommodate his longer legs. Did he care that Mia had to swiftly move her legs to the other foot well because there was now so little room in the back seat? Of course not!

They drove in silence to Autumn's office. Mia had been to this building before, but only to pick up Autumn for lunch or happy hour. She'd never actually been inside. She wanted to ask questions, figure out what was going on, what the man knew and what he wasn't telling her. He drove through the streets of Chicago and she watched his hands, unaware that she was forming silly, romantic dreams or, even worse, sexual fantasies about those hands until the sun disappeared and she blinked, coming back to the present with a thud.

CHAPTER 2

They parked in the underground parking garage and Mia took a deep breath as she followed her friend, who smiled reassuringly as they walked to the elevators, and her new lawyer, who looked like he was sucking on lemons, inside the elegant, granite and glass office building.

Stepping out of the elevators, she blinked at all the signs of wealth and success as she looked around. The law offices of The Thorpe Group were all black granite, shiny steel and sparkling glass with intelligent looking people bustling around in every direction as if they had an urgent purpose in life. Autumn had spoken of her co-workers before, but only in general terms, telling her that there were four brothers who partnered in the firm.

In Mia's mind, this wasn't a law firm. This was an enormous corporation. She had no idea how many floors each brother occupied, but it was intimidating to walk into the beautifully decorated office area wearing only jeans and a pink tee-shirt while everyone else wore immaculate, sophisticated suits with silk shirts or power ties. Mia tucked her hair behind her ears, wishing she could have put on something more sophisticated herself, or even done her hair, but she followed meekly along behind these two, wishing she were anywhere else other than following this disturbing man into his opulent office in her jeans and tee-shirt. Just a little lipstick, she thought as she stepped into the elegantly masculine room, would make her feel a bit more in control and presentable.

"Wait in here," the horrible man said, opening a door for her and waiting until she was inside before he closed it once again, with her on the inside and everyone else on the outside.

Mia stared at the closed door, her throat closing with the returning fear of being locked up for the rest of her life. Taking several deep breaths, she pushed the panic back down. She'd never been afraid of closed spaces before, but after this morning's experience, she suddenly felt clammy and nervous, as if the air around her were thicker somehow.

She backed to the center of the room and looked around, telling herself mentally that he hadn't locked her in here.

He probably thought she was guilty and should be in prison, Mia thought as she wandered around the room, concentrating on anything other than the fact that he might have locked the door. Had he put her in here to keep her from stealing the office supplies? She was being ridiculous, she knew. The door most likely locked from this side so the possibility that he'd locked her into his office was pretty low. That thought calmed her down a great deal and she was able to think more clearly.

Looking around, she noted all the various items in his office. And since he'd closed the door and told her to stay put, she wasn't above snooping. She told herself it was just her way of finding out if the man was any good at his job, but a small part of her also accepted that she wanted to know more about him personally.

The degrees on the wall caught her attention and she wandered over to look at them. Hmm…she thought, Stanford Law School. Impressive! Why were these over in the corner where most people wouldn't see them? She'd always thought people who went to the big, high-profile schools would broadcast their degrees as loudly as possible.

Wandering over behind his desk, she saw the pictures on the bookshelf. There weren't any children or women, so she assumed that Ash Thorpe wasn't married and didn't have kids. There were several pictures of four men, one of whom was Ash and the other three must be his brothers since they all looked so similar. There were several with the four men, one on a boat in crystal blue waters, another with snow falling around them, obviously a ski trip to some mountain she couldn't identify from the picture, another picture with all four men in tuxedos….she looked at each of the pictures slowly and grudgingly had to acknowledge that Ash Thorpe really was the most handsome of the group.

With a sigh, she ignored the pictures, not wanting to think of Ash Thorpe as a handsome man any longer. Looking around, she bit her lower lip and wondered how in the world she was going to be able to afford this man's hourly rate. She'd bet it was about two or three hundred dollars per hour, and there was no way she could cover that.

Of course, this was her life she was dealing with. If the man was willing to take her case, shouldn't she let him? She stared out the window but didn't see anything. Her mind was going over her assets. She had a retirement account, but she was only twenty-six so there wasn't a great deal in there yet. She could mortgage her house, but since she'd only bought it last year, there wasn't a whole lot of equity there either. In other words, she didn't have a big savings or huge assets to fall back on. These ridiculous charges were going to bankrupt her, she realized with sadness.

She'd been so careful all her life. She'd worked her way through college, saved as much as she could and bought a house because every investment expert said that real estate was the best investment. So she'd followed their advice. She'd wanted to get married and have a house full of children. Jeff had looked like the perfect candidate for a husband and father. How could she go wrong with a high school principal? But she'd slowly realized that she was going to marry him simply because she wanted the fantasy of a house and kids, not because she loved him with all her heart and soul. So she'd broken off the engagement, wanting to be honest and kind, to do the right thing so that Jeff could find someone who could love him like he deserved to be loved.

But after she'd given him back his ring, he'd gotten nasty, flinging insults at her. When she'd walked out on him during one of those conversations, he'd gotten even angrier, to the point that she'd had to block his calls on her cell phone. A month after she'd broken up with him, he'd reverted to sending her flowers, which she'd refused, candies, which she'd returned, small gifts which she'd sent back to him with a note telling him to not contact her again.

The entire fiasco had been one bad nightmare after another. She'd thought it would stop when she'd heard through one of her friends that he'd become engaged to another woman. Mia had relaxed her guard, which obviously had been a mistake. That was how she ended up here, standing in a stranger's office, snooping and fighting down panic.

She sat down in one of the comfortable chairs set up in a square by the window, her head falling into her hands as she contemplated how this was going to completely derail her life. Jeff had done this to her somehow. She didn't think he was dead. There was just something about this situation that didn't smell right and Jeff had been warning her to come back to him or he'd punish her. But for the life of her, she couldn't figure out what to do or how to prove her innocence or even her suspicion that he was behind all of this. How could she tell the police that the man they thought she'd killed probably wasn't even dead?

This was definitely a conundrum!

Ash ignored the chaos of his department, knowing that there were several high profile cases underway. Mia Paulson's case had suddenly become a higher priority, although he didn't completely understand his reaction as he walked up the stairs to the top floor. The Thorpe Group worked off of the top four floors of this building, each of his brothers having a separate floor with their staff of lawyers and support personnel filling in all the available spaces. The top floor was where his brother, Ryker, worked and was where he was headed now. He'd called an emergency meeting a moment ago and he knew that all of his brothers would drop what they were doing and get to the top floor conference room within the next five minutes.

He'd been wrong. As soon as he'd stepped into the room, his three brothers were already there.

"What's going on?" Ryker asked as soon as the door was closed. The oldest, and most emotionless, stepped forward, concern written all over his features.

"I'm taking a case pro bono," Ash said without preamble.

The three other men continued to look at Ash. "And?" one of them asked, prompting more information.

Ash was relieved. All three of his brothers were supporting him, not a single word voiced against such an action. He knew they'd always been there for each other, but this was an unusual circumstance. He wasn't even sure he could explain it to himself, much less his brothers. Ash looked at the table, his hands fisted on his lean hips. "It's a murder case where a woman is involved."

Xander crossed his arms over his chest. "Is this woman in some sort of danger?"

Ash hadn't thought of that. He knew he wasn't thinking clearly on a number of subjects, which also meant he probably shouldn't take this case. But he was going to anyway. "She isn't in danger that I know of, but I'll keep you informed as the information unfolds."

"So what's special about this case?" Axel asked, watching his brother curiously.

Ash took a deep breath before finally saying the words that might invite a different reaction but he had to be honest with his brothers. They'd never lied to each other outside of the normal sibling teasing and joshing. And he wasn't going to pussy-foot around this. Something inside of him was signaling that this was too important. "This is personal. To me."

The three men looked at their brother, stunned. "How personal?" Ryker finally asked, voicing the question they were all thinking, including Ash himself.

Ash considered his words carefully. "I don't know. My gut instinct is 'very'."

All three men thought about that. Then slowly, as they always did, nodded their heads indicating their full support. "You'll let us know how we can help," Axel came back. It wasn't a question, it was a command. The brothers were close in age, only about a year or a year and a half apart. Their parents had died in a car accident several years ago and it had brought them closer together, forming a family unit instead of letting their relationships disintegrate. Ash was the youngest at thirty-three. Axel, the next oldest, was thirty-four and always laughing about something. He was the tease in the family, but also the one that received and gave out the most poundings at the gym. They worked out together frequently in the boxing ring, a sport at which all four excelled. Xander was thirty-five and constantly fighting with their office manager, Autumn, who the three other brothers suspected that he was in love with. None of them were brave enough to step into that minefield though, afraid of the explosion that might occur. Ryker, the oldest and now the head of the family, was heading into old-man territory at thirty-six. But his old-man status wasn't because of his age, but more because he was always serious, rarely cracking a smile for anything these days.

Ash breathed a bit easier with the statement of their support and nodded, relief flooding through him. "I will. It could be a difficult case."

"And a difficult issue," Axel said, but he was starting to grin.

Ash turned to Xander, holding his brother's gaze. "She's a good friend of Autumn's as well." He wanted to give his older brother the warning and fought the urge to step backwards in case Xander exploded, which had been more often lately for some reason.

Xander immediately scowled and crossed his arms in the air. "You're going to need all of our help then," he said, implying that Autumn was the issue and not his client. "She only brings trouble."

Ash opened his mouth to say something, then looked at Axel and Ryker. Both men were thinking the same thing, but as their eyes connected, they all three decided to leave it alone.

"I've got to get back to her," he finally said. "I'll have Emma send each of you a brief on the evidence as soon as I get it from the prosecutor."

Back down on his own floor, he signaled to his investigator, Mark. "I need you to find out everything you can about these people," he said and handed him a list which contained the names of the assumed victim, the new fiancée and the very lovey Mia Paulson. "This is a rush issue. Get your team on it immediately and report back to me with whatever you can find," he ordered and Mark instantly nodded his head and moved back to his office.

Mark was one of those unassuming men who blended into all situations. But his powers of observation bordered on the supernatural and he had the best technical mind Ash had ever seen. The man could rig a camera to the most bizarre places, all to get evidence that would help their clients. He had a team of investigators that all had a scary expertise, having come from the intelligence communities or other investigative branches. Their combined expertise was worth their weight in gold because they continued to find evidence that exonerated their clients.

With the investigation starting, Ash looked towards his own office and wasn't surprised when he saw the pretty, dark head peek out of his office. He almost chuckled to himself if he hadn't felt that irritation start up again. There was just something about Mia Paulson that struck him in a way that no other female had ever done before. He couldn't define it, but he knew she had some powerful force that he wasn't going to ignore.

"Oh no, my little lady," he mumbled under his breath as he watched her pretty, grey eyes scan the room for an escape. "You aren't going anywhere."

He moved quickly and was in front of her before she even took two steps out of his office. Nudging her right back inside, he leaned against the doorway and looked down at her, amused when he saw her biting that full, pink lower lip. "Going somewhere?" he asked with a slight drawl.

Mia hid her hands behind her back. "I have to leave." At his raised eyebrow, she sighed. "Look, you're one of the best of the best," she said, pushing her hands into her pockets, unaware that the posture pulled the tee-shirt tight against her breasts, showing the hardened nipples and making his body harden as well. "I have no idea how much you charge per hour, but I simply can't afford you."

"Mia, you can't afford to walk out of this office," he said, ignoring her comment about his hourly rate.

She shook her head. "You probably charge two or three hundred dollars per hour, don't you?" she asked.

Ash shrugged one of his shoulders, her worried, grey eyes solidifying in his mind what he'd already decided earlier. "What's your point?" He didn't tell her that he charged closer to seven hundred to one thousand dollars an hour, depending on the complexity of the case. That was just his hourly rate and in her situation, it would be closer to the grand mark not to mention the hourly cost of all the investigators he'd just launched on the city as well as the support staff and the potential legal filings.

"I can't afford you. I can't raise nearly that amount of money," she explained, desperate now to get out of this office before more charges accumulated. She was so humiliated that she would even have to admit such a thing to a man like this who could probably afford anything his big heart desired.

"Mia, sit down," he commanded and walked over to his desk, indicating she should take a seat in one of the leather chairs in front of him. "Don't worry about the cost of your defense. Let's figure that out after everything is settled."

She stood there for a long moment, her mind battling with her instincts. She knew, deep down, that this man was trouble and her life would never be the same again.

He was sifting through some papers on his desk but when she continued to stand there by the door, he looked up at her. When he realized she was still worried, he walked back to stand in front of her. Taking one of her hands in his large one, he noted how cold her fingers were, and that they started trembling once again.

"I know that you're scared and not sure of what's going to happen next. But you're going to have to trust me. I'm very good at what I do, Mia. Just relax and let's take this one step at a time. You're no longer in jail, but I doubt you can work, so let's just take it slow and figure things out as they come along. Let me worry about the high level strategy and you worry about answering my questions. Does that work for you?" he asked softly, trying to reassure her but he was also fighting his instinct to pull her closer and kiss her. Instead of following on that instinct, he said, "So let's go through the issues," he suggested, trying to give her some sort of comfort but not sure how. "What was your fiancé like?" he asked, leading her over to his desk so she was sitting next to him.

Mia answered all of the man's questions, over and over again he found a detail in her story that she had to explain. People came into his office and handed him papers, which then shifted his interrogation. He was relentless in his questions, not letting her hide anything. Occasionally, someone interrupted about another case and Mia prayed that the man would give her a slight break from his interrogation, but he answered the person's question efficiently before coming right back to his questions to her. She told him about their dating relationship, the engagement, the ring, his reaction when she broke it off with him and all the small little gifts he'd sent to her, trying to convince her to come back to him.

By noon, she was exhausted. She'd been over and over the issue a million times, her fingers almost tearing her hair out. "I don't know!" she finally screamed at him. "I don't know where Jeff is! I told you, I haven't spoken to him in over a month. I threatened to put a restraining order on him because he wouldn't leave me alone!"

"And did you?"

"No!" she replied, exasperated and defeated.

"Why not?"

She sighed, shaking her head. "Because I didn't know how!" she snapped right back at him. She stood up and paced in front of the window in his office that looked out onto the Chicago skyline. "I know that sounds ridiculous to you, but normal people don't know what to do in these situations!" She was flustered that her stupidity was being brought up over and over again. "The only reason I know there's such a thing as a restraining order is because of television. But in those situations, the police are enforcing the restraining order that is already in place! The shows never explain how to actually go about putting one in place!"

She fell back down into the comfortable leather chair, bracing herself for his next question.

"Did you eat breakfast?" he asked.

Mia looked up, startled by the softer tone of his voice. When she could look at his eyes, she sighed. "No. They were too busy putting my wrists in handcuffs. They didn't give me a chance to grab my morning cereal," she replied sarcastically.

Ash thought that would be a very good look for her, but pushed that thought aside when his body instantly reacted to the visual that popped into his head. Of course, she wouldn't be clothed while the handcuffs were on. And he wouldn't be arresting her either. He cleared his throat which helped to dissipate the image a bit. "Wasn't there something offered at the jail?"

Mia looked startled by the gentleness in his voice now. "I guess so," she answered, but shrugged. "I wasn't really in the right frame of mind to grab food though."

"Come with me," Ash said, standing up and grabbing his jacket once again.

Mia stood also, but she wasn't sure she wanted to go anywhere with this man. "Where are we going?" she asked, her feet moving, but not as quickly as might be needed to keep up with his longer stride.

He looked down at her, a slight smile on his handsome face as he touched the dark circles under her eyes. "You need something to eat. And probably a few more hours of sleep, but unfortunately, that's not going to happen yet. Food, I can do. Rest is a luxury I can't offer you at this point."

Mia's shoulders drooped, but she knew he was right. "Food would be good. If you could drive me home, I can just grab a sandwich."

Ash hesitated and she looked up again. "What?" she asked, not sure if she wanted to hear what he might tell her. The look on his face promised that she wouldn't like anything he was about to say.

Ash wished he could drive her home and tuck her into her bed. He pictured her in a full sized bed with a handmade quilt draped over the top and hand embroidered pillows for decoration. She looked like the kind of woman who would embroider and quilt and he thought the idea was delightful. "You can't go home. Not yet, anyway."

Her whole body tensed with his words as well as the hard if wary look in his eyes. "Why not?"

He put a hand to the small of her back and led her out of his office. Several people handed him papers or notes and he grabbed all of them as he continued to walk out of the office. "Because your home is still being searched by the police," he said a moment before the elevator doors opened up. He nudged her inside, realizing that she was probably stunned by the news.

Mia thought about that for a moment, the news going over and over in her mind. And then it hit her. "They haven't found anything yet, have they?" she asked, her smile brightening. "That's a good thing, isn't it?"

Ash was impressed. When given that news, most people became either angry or defensive. Mia had found the bright side, which was usually what he told his clients when the police reached this point. "That's correct. It's good news."

"So they'll eventually drop the charges, right?"

He couldn't lie to her, even to give her a short period of hope. "Probably not. There is precedence where cases were tried, and the prosecution won, even when there wasn't a body. And that's what they're looking for in your yard. Apparently you have a lot of new shrubs, so the police are digging up those areas, thinking that you've buried the body in the garden."

Mia sighed, her shoulders drooping once more. She watched as his hand pressed the button to the parking garage and shook her head. "I wouldn't be so stupid as to bury anyone's body in my backyard. Not even my cats!" she grumbled.

Ash chuckled despite the seriousness of the situation. "Not even your cat's body? And why not your ex-fiancé? I thought everyone wanted their loved ones close by in the afterlife."

Mia shook her head while rolling her eyes. "Are you kidding me? Jeff bothered me enough over the past few months. If I killed him, which I didn't," she cautioned, "do you honest think I'd want him in my backyard? The obnoxious man would haunt me!"

Ash couldn't help but laugh at her logic. It might not be true, but it made sense. "You have a point," he said, his laughter subsiding to a chuckle as the doors to the elevator opened up.

He led her out of the building but, as the flashbulbs popped unexpectedly, he put his arm around Mia's shoulders protectively. His mind was frantically trying to pick up the pace and figure out what was going on.

CHAPTER 3

The crowd seemed to move in closer, blocking their way. The only reason they moved was because Ash was so much larger than they were and he was moving fast. Anyone not getting out of his way was libel to be crushed. "Has Ms. Paulson confessed to killing her fiancé?" one reporter shouted at them. "Are there any other suspects?" another called out. "She pleaded not-guilty, but why are the police digging up her yard? Do they think he's buried there?" someone else called out. All the while, the cameras were clicking away, catching Mia's stunned surprise.

Mia held onto Ash's hand, allowing him to guide her. She couldn't see a thing with all of the press gathered around them. He was more than a head taller than all of the other reporters so he could see over their heads. When he almost shoved her into a car, she didn't even care whose car it was, as long as it got her away from their cameras and questions.

Ash got into the car after her and drove away, his hands expertly handling the powerful vehicle.

After several moments, he said, "I'm sorry about that, Mia. I should have anticipated that happening."

"What was that all about?" she asked, still not sure why the press were so fired up about her case.

"You're a kindergarten teacher accused of killing your fiancé…"

"Ex-fiancé," she corrected quickly. She still didn't understand. "And don't people get accused of murder all the time? What's so special about this case?"

"The details seem to have caught the media's attention," he explained. He pressed a button on his steering wheel and a moment later, a voice came over the line. "Judy, make sure that security clears away the press in front of the building. Get a restraining order put in place for her home as well."

Mia's mouth formed a perfect "O" as she listened to him speak, ensuring that she had a clear path to her house whenever she was allowed to enter it again. "The media think I did it?" she asked weakly.

Ash didn't like the worry in her voice. She'd just started to stand up for herself a few moments ago. This was no time to get weak. "The press don't care if you did it or not. On a slow news day, anything is fair game for a story."

Mia looked out the window, shaking her head. "I teach kids," she said. "They're all young and impressionable. They won't understand what's going on, especially if the media start showing up at the school. It will scare them and be confusing. I'll lose my job over this."

Ash wasn't going to allow that. "We'll clear your name, Mia. Just hang in there."

She looked up at him, feeling his strength and power, but not sure she could trust it. "Even if you can clear my name of the criminal charges, there will always be some people out there who will think I did it."

She was right, he thought. "Then I'll just have to make sure there's no doubt in anyone's mind."

She sighed and slumped down into the soft, luxurious leather seat. "I'm not really hungry anymore. If you can just drop me off at my house," she asked.

"You can't go back there," he said again. His voice was hard and firm.

"Why not? Surely they won't be searching my house for the whole day, will they?" she asked.

"They might, depending on what they find or don't find." He considered his next words, "And even if they finish today, your house might not be habitable for a few days. Besides, we're not finished today. We have much more to do and we need your help. You're not off the hook."

He pulled into a sandwich shop and they got out. "Besides, you haven't eaten yet today. You have to grab something to eat. This is a long, tedious process and you're going to need your strength."

Mia started to follow him inside, but he waited at the front of the car for her and she felt that warm, squishy feeling in her tummy again. Darn him for being a gentleman! Why couldn't he just walk into the sandwich shop and wait for her to catch up to him like most guys? She was used to that. She could handle that. His gentlemanly manners combined with his gorgeousness were making her think and feel things that were completely inappropriate!

He even pulled out her chair for her while the waitress handed them the paper menus. She suddenly realized something and her whole face flamed with color.

"What's wrong?" he asked, instantly aware of something changing within her.

She shifted in her chair and put her menu off to the side. "Nothing," she replied nervously.

Ash's eyes narrowed towards her. "Something is wrong. Did you think of something relevant to the case?" he prompted, laying his menu down as well.

She couldn't even look at him, so horrified by her current predicament. "No. I just realized that I'm not very hungry after all."

Ash didn't believe her for a moment. "You're getting some food, Mia," he replied, his tone gentle but firm. "You haven't eaten all day and I'm going to need you alert tonight for more questions."

She sighed and closed her eyes briefly, but then her stomach betrayed her by making hunger noises. She placed her hand over her stomach and tried to play it off. "I'm just nervous that's all. It isn't every day a girl gets arrested," she said, pretending to laugh but the sound was more nervous than humorous.

Ash suspected what was wrong and tried not to smile. "How about a bowl of New England clam chowder and a Rueben sandwich?" he suggested. "Or a burger with extra cheese and onion rings?" he asked, watching her carefully. When her mouth dropped open slightly with the second option, he put his menu down with a satisfied nod. "Burger it is, then," he said and signaled to the waitress who had been standing by the counter waiting for him to be ready.

"No! Really. I'm fine."

Ash looked at the waitress and ordered their cheeseburgers with onion rings and an extra side of French fries. "Can you bring some vinegar with that as well?" he asked.

Of course the waitress nodded her ascent, eager to rush off and do his bidding as quickly as possible. Mia glared at the woman, wanting to spit when the hussy swayed her hips in an obvious invitation.

Mia looked back at the man, wanting to see if he was ogling the waitress. She needed something to calm these crazy feelings that were swimming through her mind. But the man wasn't watching the waitress! He was watching her watching the waitress. And was that amusement on those firm, sexy lips?

"I don't have my wallet," she finally admitted, needing to throw him off the scent of her jealousy over the waitress and onto new territory.

"I figured that out," he laughed. "Did you think I was going to make you buy your own meal?"

She glanced down at her fingers which were tangled tightly together on her lap, nervous with those blue eyes on her once again. "I'm not sure what I'm thinking today. It's been one of those crazy, unpredictable days that I hope never to experience again."

He chuckled softly. "And I'm here to make sure this one blows over quickly enough." He paused a moment, looking at her soft, worried and tired eyes. "Do you really save earthworms?" he asked, unable to stop the question once it popped into his mind.

She looked up at him, not sure what he was talking about. "Save earthworms?" she repeated, confused.

"Autumn was telling me what a stellar human being you were as she was pushing me out of my office to get to the courthouse faster. One of the things she said as a way to convince me of your innocence was your need to save earthworms from the heat of the sun."

Mia flushed and looked down again. She wasn't exactly sure what she could say, but she shrugged her shoulders slightly. "I don't like to see them suffering," she said in almost a whisper.

The possibility that earthworms had the ability to actually experience pain and suffering struck him and he threw back his head and laughed. He knew he was making her uncomfortable and he tried to hide his amusement, but every time he looked down at her from across the table, the laughter started up again. He couldn't help it. She was so cute and actually sincere about her need to save the same worms that he and his brothers speared onto hooks whenever they went fishing.

Thankfully, their burgers arrived at that moment and she was able to hide her flushed cheeks behind the burger which actually tasted fantastic, despite her worry over her current legal problems. He let her get halfway through her burger and fries before he started in on the questions again. This time, she wasn't sure why he was asking some of the questions, but she answered them as honestly as she could. But they were things like what her favorite color was, were her parents still alive and why she'd chosen teaching as opposed to a profession that might be more lucrative.

"We can't all be dynamo lawyers and billionaires, can we?" she asked with a smile, used to people wondering why she chose teaching. "It isn't a big secret," she explained, wiping her fingers on her napkin. "I love the kids. I love seeing them learn. When they enter my classroom at the beginning of the school year, most of them don't know how to read and can barely identify the alphabet. By the end of the year, they're excited to read me books, some have started math skills, and they are more confident and eager to please. It's just an exciting process," she said to him and then grabbed the last onion ring, not even sorry either.

He looked back at her with a blank look and she wondered what he was thinking. Most people thought she was crazy to be stuck in a room with twenty-five to thirty kids. They pictured a room filled with chaos and screams but that wasn't the way it was. She had fun with her students

They drove back to the office and Mia wearily followed him back to the elevator, grateful that all the reporters had left the area, but still nervous about whatever additional questions he might have for her. She'd never talked about herself as much as she had today and it made her uncomfortable.

Once inside the building, she shifted over to the other side of the elevator, feeling odd when she was too close to the man. She knew he didn't like her and it irritated her beyond anything to know that. There was something about this man that struck her deeply, made her feel….okay, this was cliché, but he made her feel weak in the knees. Him buying her a burger and fries didn't help either. Most men were horrified by how much she could eat but this guy, he just looked at her with admiration.

She just needed to keep telling herself that he didn't believe in her innocence. He was working this case because it was his job and he was getting paid an incredible amount of money to get her out of jail and keep her out. He didn't care about her innocence or guilt. He just cared about the next almighty dollar and how many hours he could bill against her poor, beleaguered bank account.

As she stepped out of the elevator, she turned so that he couldn't touch her back. Her body might think he was the sexiest man alive but her mind recoiled at the idea of any man who didn't think she was good and honest, and more importantly, not a murderess, to touch her.

Ash's eyebrow went up as she turned so as to ensure that he couldn't touch her. Fine, he thought with irritation. She wasn't even his type. He preferred blonds, he told himself. Tall, leggy blonds!

So what if he couldn't keep his eyes off of her adorable, sexy derriere? And he wasn't actually staring at her long legs, wondering what it would be like to slide his hand down her calf, see if the back of her knee was ticklish.

Ash shifted his belt buckle slightly as he led her into the conference room where everyone was already assembled. She started to take a seat over by the conference room wall but he grabbed her arm and forced her to sit next to him. Why the hell he cared where she sat was a mystery he wasn't going to think about. He just wanted the damn woman where he could see her. Call it suspicion or maybe even an instinct for survival. He was going with his gut this time around. To hell with logic.

"Okay everyone, settle down," he called out to the assembled group. He didn't want to stifle their thought processes, but he needed those thoughts organized and going in the same direction. "We have a new face in the group. If you haven't met her already, please introduce yourselves to Kiera Ward. If you haven't heard about the case she just won in California, well, then you're fired because you should be keeping up with all court cases no matter where they were tried," he said and the rest of the group laughed. "Don't let her age confuse you. She's a hard hitter who brings passion and a dedication to the team that is admirable. Her ability to win cases in several high profile trials recently will be an asset to our team. Don't be shy and make sure you include her in the progress of this trial." Obviously all of them had heard about the case so he moved on. "What do we have?"

Ash remained standing at the head of the table while the rest of his investigative and legal team briefed him on their progress of the morning.

Mark, the lead investigator, stood up and read from his notes. "First of all, there's the assumed victim's blood on a baseball trophy with Ms. Paulson's fingerprints all over it. The police have bagged it but I'm trying to get the placement of the fingerprints to determine hold."

Mia glanced up to see Ash's expression. He looked just as hard and tough as normal, no reaction to the fact that her fingerprints were on what everyone assumed was the murder weapon.

She spoke up, trying to offer help wherever possible. "I know that trophy. Jeff showed it to me when we were first dating," she interrupted and felt nervous now that all eyes were on her. "It was his pride and joy," she explained.

"That's a good explanation for how your fingerprints got onto the trophy. Mark will get more information on the placement."

She bit her lip, confused but afraid of speaking up again. She wasn't one who liked the spotlight and this was an intimidating group of men and women.

Ash noticed the change in her eyes and reacted to it. He wouldn't normally slow down to explain with so many people here, but he seemed to be doing everything differently with this woman. Including wanting her so badly he was tempted to order everyone out of the conference room so he could finally kiss her and taste those lips of hers that she kept biting. He wanted to bite them himself, see how soft they were and….

Getting off track, he reminded himself once again. "The placement of the fingerprints can show that you were holding it in a certain way. If you were to grab it at the top so that the heavy bottom side could strike the victim's head, that would be different than if your fingerprints were at the bottom of the trophy. That would indicate that you were holding it to look at it instead of using it as a weapon."

Mia smiled, grateful for his explanation but her mind instantly went back to the moment when she'd been holding it. She tried to picture it in her mind and she was relatively sure that she'd held it at both the top and the bottom, knowing how proud Jeff was about the trophy and not wanting to break it or drop it.

Ash was already onto the next problem with her defense. He turned back to Mark, nodding for him to continue with his discoveries. "The most obvious issue, the assumed victim has been missing for more than a week. He hasn't called in sick to work, none of his co-workers have heard from him, he just didn't show up. There's been no visible movement at his house, according to the neighbors I spoke with this morning, but that doesn't mean much since it doesn't appear that anyone really knew the guy much. The neighbors don't seem to be the type to socialize with each other."

Mia agreed with that. It had been one of the fights they'd gotten into during their relationship several times. She'd hated his neighborhood and he'd fought hard to keep her from buying her little cottage. But she'd fallen in love with both the house and the neighbors even before she'd moved in so she'd ignored his suggestion to save her money for something bigger.

Again, Ash didn't show any type of reaction to the news that Jeff was gone, missing and hadn't been seen. He didn't even look in her direction for her reaction.

Oooh! She really was starting to hate that man. But how could one like a guy who thought she'd killed her ex-fiancé?

"What else?" he prompted, writing something down on his notebook.

Mark signaled to another investigator. "A co-worker at Ms. Paulson's school gave a statement to the police that Ms. Paulson and the assumed victim were fighting on several occasions. No one heard what the conversations were about, but they explained that the arguments were heated."

Ash finally turned to Mia, one dark eyebrow arrogantly raised as if to declare that it was finally her turn to explain the circumstances. She sat up straighter in her chair, feeling nervous now that all of these confident and educated people were waiting for her to explain. "I can only think that the arguments were when I demanded that Jeff stop stalking me. I'd asked him repeatedly to leave me alone after our breakup but he was determined to try and convince me to give him another chance."

"What was the breakup about?" Ash demanded, turning to lean against the conference room table, his huge arms crossed over his chest, straining the material over those bulging biceps.

Mia shrugged. "I guess we, or perhaps just me, felt that the relationship wasn't going anywhere."

Again, without a word, he tilted his head, urging her to continue.

Mia sighed and slapped her thighs. "Jeff just became too demanding. He wanted…things, that I didn't feel we were ready for."

She felt as much as saw Ash's body stiffen. "You mean you…"

"Stop right there!" she snapped. She was glaring right back at the man. "My personal relationship with Jeff is not an issue here."

Ash shook his head and walked over to her. Without an explanation, he grabbed her arm and pulled her out of the conference room and into a smaller, empty conference room right across the hallway.

As soon as the door was closed, he turned to face her, looking stern and commanding. "Let's get something straight right now, Mia. Everything about your personal life is an issue now. Every detail is going to be dragged through the mud and through court. If this goes to trial, you can damn well expect that the prosecutor is going to ask it. He or she is going to try and make you squirm and if that means dragging your sex life through the mud, then that's going to happen."

He waited a moment to let that statement sink in before he continued. "So what was it that Jeff was asking you to do in the bedroom that you refused to do?"

"Nothing!" she gasped back, her hand covering her neck in shock.

Ash ran a hand through his hair. "What? Did he want you to dress up like a French maid and dust him off?"

"No!"

"Leather and chains?"

"No!"

"Whips? Bondage?"

"Absolutely not!"

"What the hell was it?"

"Nothing!" she snapped, disgusted by the idea of even considering doing any of those things with Jeff.

Ash rolled his eyes, his hands fisted on his hips and he glared down at her. "Mia, what was it that you wouldn't do in the bedroom with Jeff? I can tell that this is the pink elephant in the room."

"Nothing!" she yelled back at him, her hands pushing her hair out of her eyes. "Nothing okay? Nothing at all! I wouldn't sleep with him, I wouldn't have sex with him, I wouldn't do anything beyond kissing him and in the end, even that creeped me out. Okay? So nothing! The problem is that I wouldn't do anything with the jerk, okay?"

Ash looked down at her, trying to understand. "Wouldn't do what?" he asked again. He had an inkling, but it was so impossible, he couldn't conceive of it.

Mia crossed her arms over her chest, trying to suppress the anger and embarrassment she was feeling as this tall, gorgeous and obviously very sexually active man continued to stare down at her like she was some sort of weirdo.

"I wouldn't have sex!" she said, it again. "How else can I explain it? I didn't have sex with him! I know, I'm ridiculous. But I'm not a control freak. I just…" She shrugged, not sure how she could explain that she hadn't ever wanted to have sex, not even with a man who she'd agreed to marry.

"Not ever? Or just not with your ex?" he clarified. He told himself that it probably wasn't important for the case. But something inside of him knew it was extremely important to him.

Mia couldn't look at him. She turned slightly to the side and stared at the blank wall. "Not ever."

There was a long, painful silence while Mia waited for this terrifying man to start laughing at her. Her whole body tensed for that to happen which is exactly what Jeff had done when she'd told him. And once he'd stopped laughing, he wanted to know if she was mal-formed or if she was ashamed of her body.

She hated this. She wished she'd just gone ahead and had sex with one of her boyfriends in college. There had been ample opportunity. And it wasn't like she was opposed to sex. She just wanted it to mean something. She wanted to be swept away by the passion and desperate for the man to touch her. She didn't want it to be a strained, awkward activity. And she definitely didn't want to have sex with a man simply to prove to him that she was attracted to him, which was why she eventually broke things off with Jeff. He told her she had to have sex with him to prove that she loved him or he was walking away. So she let him walk.

But Ash didn't say a word. They stood facing each other, Mia looking straight at his chest while she waited tensely for his amusement and ridicule. "Okay then. Let's get back to the meeting," he said and walked back through the door, holding it open for her.

Mia couldn't believe it. Wasn't he going to laugh? Wasn't he going to question her further? Demand details? Tell her she was a freak?

She wasn't going to press it. She walked through the doorway and back into the conference room where the conversations automatically stopped. Everyone turned back to Ash, waiting for his next line of questioning.

Mia wanted to kiss him when he simply moved on to the next problem. He didn't bring up anything she'd just said or offer any sort of explanation. "Okay, Mark, you're in charge of the baseball trophy. I'll interview Mia's co-workers to see what they can give us. Ann," he called out to another investigator, "Go to the high school where Jeff worked and find out details of his work life." He looked around the room. "What else do we have?" he asked.

People started calling out various ideas and Ash nodded his head in approval or shifted their focus slightly. Mia listened, more in awe of his processes than she had been earlier in the day when he'd gotten her out of jail without any bail. The man was a powerhouse and she was pretty impressed. He commanded the room with fairness but complete authority. She could see that everyone who was working this case was impressed with how he worked. All were eager to shift their direction when he suggested a new course and proud when he approved of where they were already going.

They'd been brainstorming for about two hours and the afternoon was starting to shift towards evening when two other men came in and sat down towards the back of the room. A third man came in a few minutes later and she wiggled uncomfortably as they surveyed her while Ash and his team continued to throw out ideas. She answered everyone's questions, not really sure why they might be asking some of them, but she gave as much information as she could.

About an hour later, Mia was dragging even though everyone else in the room was still going strong. "That should be it," he called out to everyone.

People unhurriedly stood up, stretching after such a long meeting as they gathered up their things and slowly shuffled out the door. The three men towards the back remained and, when everyone else was gone, they stood up and moved towards Ash. The closer they came, the more nervous she became. And she could also see the resemblance between the four men, which meant they were the other Thorpe brothers. Their reputations were fearsome and she could feel herself moving slightly closer to Ash, although she wasn't completely conscious of what she was doing. She only knew that she felt safer now that she was a few inches closer to his enormous body.

"What are the odds?" one of them asked as they came closer.

Ash shifted, subtly letting his brothers know that she was his. Staking his claim seemed like such a primitive action, but he felt primitive right now and he wasn't going to apologize for it. Nor was he going to delve into the reasons for that feeling right at the moment. She'd moved away from him before the meeting but she was shifting towards him now. And that was all the subtle signs he needed to go caveman with his brothers.

He put a hand to the small of her back, his body reacting when she moved even closer to him, almost leaning against his side unconsciously. "Mia, these ugly men are my brothers," he explained. "This is Ryker. He's the oldest and most boring," he said, referring to the one that looked the most serious. Mia shook his hand, but moved right back to Ash's side. "And this is Xander, the next oldest and most cynical," he waited while Mia shook Xander's hand carefully, "and Axel, the most irritating."

Mia shook each man's hand, hoping her smile appeared more sincere than it felt. It occurred to her that she didn't have the same reaction to their touch as she did when Ash touched her. When that happened, it felt like a lightning bolt shot through her body. She was left confused and disoriented not to mention her mind going in strange, embarrassing directions. All three men were staring at her as if trying to dissect her and she wanted to punch Ash's arm for being so rude. She felt he should say something like, "She's innocent." Or maybe "We're going to get the charges dropped soon." Instead, he just stood there discussing the case while silently telling his brothers some weird male message that she couldn't decipher.

"Sounds like a good strategy," Ryker said. "But you know she can't go home."

Mia looked from one to the other and they were all nodding.

Ash looked down at her to explain. "Your house and yard have been locked off as a potential crime scene. They claim they haven't finished looking for your ex's body yet so they won't allow you back in."

Her eyes widened. "They've been at it all day. What have they found that could possibly lead them to assume he still might be hidden in there somewhere? It's a pretty small house too. Only two bedrooms, one bathroom, a kitchen, and a family room. I don't even have a formal dining room!"

"It's an old house, from what I understand. You have a basement."

Mia waited, wondering where he was going with that. "And?" she prompted when he didn't continue.

"And there's fresh cement apparently."

She thought carefully, trying to remember what was in the basement. He was right, it was an old house but the basement had been stone before. The previous owners had cemented over the basement because of leaks during the spring rainy season. "But I didn't put the cement down," she exclaimed when she realized what they were thinking. "It was there before I moved in. I don't even know if it was the previous owners or the ones before that."

Ash leaned against the table again. "It doesn't matter. They can't tell the age of the cement. So they're trying to determine if anything is buried underneath."

She almost fell into the chair behind her. "So they have a jackhammer in my basement destroying the foundation. Great." She wasn't sure what she was going to do now. It sounded like her whole house was being completely destroyed brick by stone. "Okay, so I'll..." she thought quickly, trying to figure out what she was going to do. "I'll just stay in a hotel until this blows over. It won't be long, right?" she looked up at Ash, fighting tears and begging him to tell her that he would overcome this situation quickly. She didn't even care if it was a lie at this point. She just needed to hear him say it. If he said it, she could believe it. The man was too big and too strong for anyone to contradict him, right?

Ash saw the tears she was valiantly fighting and his gut twisted. "Yes. We'll get this all resolved quickly. But I doubt you can afford a hotel. So you'll stay with me."

Four sets of surprised eyes looked at Ash. He shifted uncomfortably, but he wasn't backing down. "She can stay in the spare bedroom. There's plenty of room." He said this as if it was the most obvious and common sense approach, but Mia was already shaking her head.

"I can watch out for myself," she said. "There's a hotel down the street from me."

Ash turned to face her, effectively blocking out his brothers. "Mia, two streets in any direction in your neighborhood and you're driving into gang violence or a highway. The hotels in your area might not be expensive, but they're probably filled with crawling characters you don't want to run into. And I'm not just talking about the eight legged kind either." He let that sink in a moment before he continued. "You can't stay in your house and you're not staying in a hotel that you can't afford or you might not come out of alive."

She still shook her head, refusing to budge on this issue. "I'm not staying with you."

"She can stay with me," Ryker offered.

Both Axel and Xander actually took a step backwards with that offer. But Ryker continued to stare back at his youngest brother, the offer still out there and amusement in his darker blue eyes.

"No way in hell," Ash growled, his hands fisting by his sides as he struggled to keep himself from punching his oldest brother. Ryker might be the serious and conservative member of the family, but that didn't stop him from enjoying the ladies. In fact, they swarmed to him, all of them eager to spend his money and ease his frustrations.

Someone cleared his throat with the rising tension. "I'm sure Autumn would let her stay with her," Axel piped up.

Ash turned to glare at his brothers, irritated that they were even butting in. Unfortunately, Autumn probably would be more than happy to offer her best friend a place to stay. It infuriated Ash that he couldn't easily refute that option.

"Autumn has book club tonight," Xander offered.

The three brothers all turned their attention to Xander, all of them wondering how the man knew Autumn's evening schedule so well but none were willing to ask the question. Each of them shook their heads and suppressed their curiosity. "She's staying with me," Ash countered. "Come on," he told her, grabbing her hand before anyone else could offer a solution that would actually work. He had no idea why it was so important to make sure that Mia was under his roof tonight. He just knew that it was and he was going to get out of here before anything changed.

"Get your purse," he grumbled. "Someone from the office went to your house and was able to get you some clothes, your purse, keys and wallet. They are in my office."

He reached inside the door and pulled out a duffle bag, slung it over his shoulder then continued to the elevators, keeping her hand in his the whole time.

The touch of his hands immediately sent her mind going in crazy directions and she couldn't focus for a moment. She'd never had this kind of a reaction when Jeff touched her, or any of her previous boyfriends. So why did this man's touch affect her so dramatically? Why was it that the one man who thought she might be a criminal was also the one that sent such a spark through her body?

Needing a break from his closeness, if only for one night, she thought to try one more argument so that she wasn't sleeping in his home tonight. "I'm pretty sure that Autumn won't be going to her book club tonight," Mia said, almost running to keep up with the man in the strange mood. "I'm in the same book club and all of the other members are friends of mine. They won't meet without me."

Ash pressed the elevator button and stared straight ahead. "Then she's probably there talking to your friends and getting their support, trying to figure out what happened to your ex. So she's working and we shouldn't disturb her."

Mia thought he might be right and bit her lower lip, trying to come up with a counter argument. "I should probably be there as well, to answer their questions. Then I can go home with Autumn afterwards."

"You'll come home with me and we'll go over the details one more time. Maybe something will come to you over dinner."

Mia sighed, knowing that he was right there. Every time someone had mentioned an issue the police had found, she'd been able to give them something to investigate, something to check into that might shed some light on why the police were pursuing her so vehemently.

Thankfully, the security guards had kept the press away so there weren't any cameras flashing in her eyes this time around. He tucked her into the passenger seat of his car and she was once again struck by how much money Ash must make to be able to afford a vehicle so amazingly luxurious.

Well, he defended criminals, charged them exorbitant rates and basically circumvented the justice system.

That probably wasn't a fair assessment of his skills. But he was so big and so intimidating, she didn't feel like being fair. She watched him walk around the front of his car, her eyes fascinated by his long legs and her mind trying to determine what was underneath his expensive suit. She couldn't believe her mind was going in that direction! It was so….naughty and she was never naughty!

She didn't like him one bit. And she continued to tell herself that the whole way home. She repeated the statement as he showed her through his gorgeous brownstone where he occupied all four floors of a beautiful townhouse in one of the older sections of Chicago. It was a quiet neighborhood with old, oak trees shading the sidewalks and elaborate, black bannisters leading up to a newly renovated home. Inside, the brick was still showing and he'd even pulled away the ceiling to show the raw wooden support beams, giving the place an edgy but comfortable feeling.

Ash watched her out of the corner of his eye as she entered his house, wanting to see her reaction. He loved this place. He had bought it several years ago and done most of the work himself. Of course, he could always count on his brothers to help when there was heavy lifting needed. Or when one of them wanted to burn off some stress from the office. For some reason he wasn't going to delve into too deeply, her reaction was extremely important to him.

When he noticed her eyes widen as she took in the main living area with the deep sofas and the rough looking floorboards, he wasn't sure if that was good or bad. But when she saw the large windows that looked out into the back yard with the deck and landscaping, she smiled and his shoulders relaxed somewhat.

"You can stay in here," he said, dumping the duffle bag inside the doorway of a comfortable looking bedroom that looked like a designer had created the space. "Why don't you freshen up and meet me out in the kitchen? I'll cook something for dinner and we can talk some more."

Mia was left alone for the first time since she'd been rudely woken up this morning. She just stood there for a moment, absorbing the silence. She didn't think about her own home or what she would or should be doing now. She refused to let her mind start worrying about her students and what they might be thinking about after hearing of her arrest. She focused only on relaxing her mind.

Focusing on the here and now, she looked around at the large, comfortable room. Someone obviously used the room because there were shirts and suits in the closet. Ash probably let his brothers crash at his place when they went out partying or something. She didn't really care. She was just grateful for the silence.

She went to the bathroom and washed her hands and face, feeling marginally better. When she looked into the duffel bag he'd dumped by the door for her, she found a pair of black slacks and a white blouse along with underwear. She hoped that Autumn had gone to her place and gotten these items because she couldn't imagine someone else going through her personal items. As she dug through her makeup, she was sure of it. Only Autumn would know which lipsticks were her favorite and how much she loved to brush her teeth. Whenever she was stressed, Mia brushed her teeth. The clean, minty feeling helped her feel more in control.

She did that now and felt even better but she knew what would relax her even more thoroughly. She didn't have her workout clothes, but she slipped her running shoes off along with her socks and centered herself in the middle of the room. Taking several deep breaths, she closed her eyes, then slowly leaned forward, letting her arms hang down to the floor with her knees straight. The stretch in her back muscles and on the back of her thighs was instant and relaxing. She let everything unwind from her waist upwards, or downwards since she was hanging down, her hands resting on the floor.

She moved from one yoga pose to the next, feeling the tension slowly seep out of her muscles. She went into cobra pose, her eyes closed and her face facing up to the ceiling, then shifting all of her weight back into downward dog.

Ash pulled out all the ingredients for dinner, opened a bottle of wine and got down the wine glasses. He normally drank beer when at home, but he didn't think Mia was the kind of woman who would appreciate a good lager. She struck him as more of a merlot kind of lady.

Several minutes later, when she still hadn't come downstairs, he started to worry about her. She'd been through a stressful, horrible day. Mia seemed too fragile to endure what she'd gone through today, but she'd rallied, answering all of his questions, enduring the arrest, the reporters, his staff shooting ideas and questions towards her. And she'd done it all with grace and patience. He'd never had a more cooperative client before. And she'd done it all while looking like the most desirable woman he'd ever seen.

What if she were upstairs, finally cracking under the pressure? She'd gone through so much, what if she were crying? What if she were struggling to get through the evening?

He didn't like where his thoughts were going. His mouth compressed into a grim line as he looked up the stairway to the opening above. When she still didn't emerge with her bright, happy smile like he wanted her to, he tossed the dish rag down onto the counter and strode across the combined kitchen and great room to the stairs. Taking them two at a time, Ash hurried to the room where he'd left her, his imagination making him increase the pace substantially. He hoped she wasn't the kind of woman who would do something stupid. Were there any sharp objects in his bathroom? He knew his brothers used the room when one of them stayed overnight, so there could be razors in the drawers. That thought had him almost sprinting down the hallway.

The sight that greeted him as he stood in the doorway was the farthest thing he could have imagined. Strike that! He couldn't have imagined this in any way.

Mia wasn't slitting her wrists or knotting bed sheets to hang herself from the rafters. She wasn't even sitting on the bed or in the middle of the floor sobbing her heart out. She was standing on the hardwood floor, doing possibly the most erotic moves he'd ever witnessed. In the back of his mind, he suspected she was doing yoga. But he wasn't in the right frame of mind to be rational about what she was doing. His whole body froze – except for one important part of him, and that was the part that was thinking right now. Okay, so thinking wasn't exactly the right term for what it was doing. Reacting was a better term.

She moved slowly. His eyes followed the curve of her neck, the arch of her spine and the way that arch pressed her breasts against her tee-shirt. Then she moved again, her body folding upwards, ending with her bottom in the air! Were her legs really that long? And damn if she didn't fold herself forward one more time, moving into yet another position.

"What the hell are you doing?" Ash demanded, desperately needing to either join in or stop her from going to another pose. He didn't think she would appreciate the positions he'd put her into if he joined her. But his feet wouldn't move so he could back away and give her some privacy, which is what he knew he should do if he were a gentleman. So the only option was to stop her from doing anything else.

Mia's body jerked out of downward dog and she tried to stop her fall, but couldn't quite manage it. She toppled gracelessly onto the floor with a loud "Hmph!" Seeing him standing there, his jacket and tie off, his tailored shirt unbuttoned down to the middle of his chest and his sleeves rolled up revealed the strong muscles on his forearms. What was a woman to do?

She pulled herself up and dusted her bottom, glaring up at him. "Yoga!" she snapped back at him. "What did it look like?"

"Torture," he calmly replied. Or the sexiest thing he'd ever seen in his life, he thought as he looked down at her indignant expression. "Feel better?" he asked, trying to suppress the laughter as she rubbed her cute, little bottom where she'd fallen on it a moment ago.

"I was. Until you rudely interrupted me." She took a deep breath and realized how rude she sounded. "I apologize. You're going out of your way to help me and I'm just being snarky. Thank you very much for putting me up for the night. I promise to be out of your house tomorrow. No matter what happens."

He didn't respond for a moment, just stared down at her. "We'll see," he finally replied. "Let's eat."

Ash walked back to the kitchen, painfully aware that she was following him. His body was already hard and ready for her, his jaw clenching with the need to touch her soft cheek, to see if those tender lips tasted as good as they looked. And he wanted to fill his hands up with her full, luscious breasts and test their weight, feel the hard points that he could see through her tee-shirt with his thumb and watch her reaction.

Damn! He was just making it worse.

But he'd probably help her relax a hell of a lot more than doing yoga! Or maybe it would just help him relax! He certainly wasn't relaxed watching her doing yoga. And he was fairly sure that men's bodies didn't move like she'd been moving, nor did he want to attempt any of those poses. Maybe he should just call up one of his brothers and tell him to meet him at the gym. A good boxing match would do the trick since he couldn't touch the lovely lady sitting primly across the counter from him.

He moved behind the island until he could get his body back under control. To occupy his mind, he poured her a glass of red wine. "I hope you like pasta," he said more gruffly than he'd intended as he lifted the glass to hand it to her. He cleared his throat, trying to get a grip on his raging lust. But every time he thought he might have it under control, he looked at her, saw her soft curls dancing around her pretty face and he pictured her in one of those damn yoga poses again!

"I love pasta," she said evenly, oblivious to his lust-filled state of mind, slipping onto one of the odd looking chairs warily. She was surprised when it was much more comfortable than it looked. "This is really nice," she said, taking a sip of the wine and looking around. "Who was your designer?" she asked, looking at the beams above her, the rough, brick wall and the enormous fireplace over in the corner that was so big, she suspected it would still be able to heat the kitchen area on a cold, winter's afternoon.

"I did it all myself," he replied, taking a plate and spooning an enormous pile of pasta onto the center. He then ladled rich, fragrant red sauce, topping it all with a handful of cheese. "Dig in."

Mia looked at the enormous amount of food he'd given her. It was about the same amount she would make whenever she cooked pasta, but she would also divide this up into four portions, freezing the other three for future dinners that she could easily heat up in the microwave. "Goodness, this is a lot of food." She tried not to laugh at his grim face, but she couldn't help a bit of the amusement she was feeling at his serving sizes. Amazingly, he served himself more than twice what he'd given her.

He took the chair next to her, ignoring her laughter as he pointed towards her plate, indicating she should eat up. "You've had a lot of stress today. You're going to need the energy to regroup."

She laughed softly. "That's sort of what yoga does," she replied back, but picked up her fork.

Ash mentally disagreed with her. Mia Paulson doing yoga definitely did not reduce his stress level. In fact, his stress level was pretty high right about now despite his attempts to calm down.

To help distract himself, he opened her file and read through the details. As they ate, he asked her questions. But when she answered, their conversation diverged and he asked her more personal questions than he would ask of his other clients. The conversation ended up being less about the case and more about him just learning about who she was as a person. And he was surprised to find her funny and intelligent.

Mia couldn't believe how relaxed she was just sitting here talking with him. Once there was a lull in his questions and she piped up, eager to gain her own insight into the man she'd been around for what seemed like days or even weeks although it was only hours. She sipped her wine and worked on whittling down the enormous pile of pasta he'd given her while she asked him questions about how he'd renovated this building on his own. She loved listening to him talk with his deep voice sending shivers along her skin with awareness. He seemed so competent in the legal areas, and yet he had this whole other side of him. She discovered that he liked cooking and working with his hands, explaining that it was the complete opposite of what he did all day long.

"It helps me work through the legal issues."

She thought about that for a moment, thinking that it made sense. "Sort of like occupying one side of your mind with the mundane while the other side is occupied with working through a problem," she suggested.

"I suppose that's one way to put it," he agreed.

She smiled. "I do that with my kids. After recess, I give them a craft project to work on. While their little hands are busy cutting and gluing pieces of a puzzle or a craft, I give them facts about history or science. I'm always amazed at how much they actually absorb during these periods. One would think that they were distracted with the craft materials and, to a point, they are. But our minds can process more than one thing if the distractions work together with the facts."

He was impressed. But then his eyes looked down at her lips one more time and he was once again lost in the idea of tasting those lips. Of feeling them tremble underneath his. He knew she would tremble too. He had no idea how he knew that. It was just a sense or maybe a vibe.

He was just about to lean forward and test his theory. But he stopped himself, suddenly realizing that she was his client. And she was terrified of what she was facing. He couldn't take advantage of her fragility right now. No matter how soft and sexy she looked, Mia Paulson was off limits.

"You must be tired," he said and stood up abruptly. He picked up both of their plates, noting absently that she'd eaten barely any of the pasta and only drank half a glass of wine. "Can I make you anything else?" he asked as he put the plates in the sink.

"Goodness, no!" Mia said, feeling awkward now. She'd been hoping that he would bend over and kiss her. But why on earth would she want that? This man didn't respect her at all! He thought she was a murderer.

He must have remembered that little issue and pulled back, repulsed by the idea of even touching her. "I will do the dishes," she offered, needing to pay him back in some small way for his hospitality.

"I have a housekeeper who comes in each morning and cleans up. She'll do the dishes," he countered. "Why don't you head to bed? I'll lock up." He was wiping his hands on a dishtowel, using it to keep his hands from reaching out and grabbing her, pulling her against him and kissing her until she was gasping for breath. He only stopped himself because he could see the dark circles under her eyes and her smile wasn't quite as bright as it had been this morning.

Then there was also that irritating little issue: he had to remind himself over and over how unethical it would be to kiss her!

Mia watched him for a long, painful moment, wishing he would wrap those big, strong arms around her and kiss her, make her forget all of the mess her life had become over the last eighteen hours. She shouldn't want him, and this crazy fluttering she kept experiencing was probably just because he looked so strong and capable. And she needed someone to reassure her today. No, it was probably nothing, but her emotions were teetering on the brink and she should just leave right now before she did something crazy. Like throw herself into his arms.

When she saw the distance in his eyes, she knew she should be relieved. She didn't like him. And he didn't like her. So why did she feel like crying simply because the man wouldn't kiss her?

She turned around and headed towards the bedroom he was loaning her for the night, but she paused. "Thank you very much," she said with one hand on the steel bar that acted as a railing for the architectural-like stairs, staring back at him from the distance for a long moment.

She walked slowly up the stairs and turned down the hallway, feeling like it was a march of shame. She should have just stayed away. Why had she silently begged him to kiss her? Was she slowly losing her mind? Today had been horrible, she thought as she brushed her teeth and slid into the bed. In fact, of all the bad days she'd experienced in her life, this one ranked just below the day her parents had died. She missed them terribly right now.

She pulled off her clothes, refusing to let the tears flow. She just had to get through this day one moment at a time. She should listen to Ash's advice because she knew he was the best. Financial issues aside, he was right. She should figure out how to save herself before she worried about how she was going to pay for him saving her.

With a sigh, she slunk down under the covers, impressed by how comfortable the bed was and how soft the sheets were. His housekeeper had good taste, she thought as she stared up at the ceiling. And he even knew how to cook! She smiled at his worried expression earlier when she was able to eat only a quarter of the enormous amount of food he'd given her. But she'd continued to sip the wine, downing a whole glass tonight. The alcohol had helped her relax and she definitely felt better with the extra carbs from the pasta.

CHAPTER 4

Ash heard the door click closed and was instantly awake. It was just after midnight! Where could the woman be going at this time of the night?

Several ideas occurred to him, one of which was to hide any evidence in her home that the police hadn't yet discovered. He probably should have been more concerned with her breaking the law to save herself. But the only thing he thought in that moment was to stop her from going home, because the police were surely there, waiting for her to come home. He couldn't let that happen!

Sitting up in bed, he listened carefully for a long moment but when he didn't hear anything else, he cursed under his breath and threw the covers off. Pulling on a pair of jeans and some old running shoes, he only took another second to grab a shirt, pulling it over his shoulders before sprinting down the hallway. He glanced in her bedroom and sure enough, the covers were pulled back and the bed was empty.

With another curse, he raced down the hallway, hoping he didn't break his ankle or trip over anything in the dark house. The building was only four stories so, instead of waiting for the elevator to come back up, he took the stairs down, hopping from level to level. If she was going out meeting with someone, trying to hide evidence or even out killing someone else, he was damn sure going to stop her. He dismissed from his mind the fact that he'd assumed she was innocent. He'd told people over and over again that looks could be deceiving and he wasn't going to let his libido control this situation. Just because he wanted to bed her didn't mean she was automatically innocent. No one was as innocent as Mia appeared to be. No one was that naïve either!

Damn her! She'd half convinced him that she was all that and a cupcake and here she was, sneaking out at midnight going who knows where. No one snuck out at midnight to do anything innocent which meant he was going to somehow stop her from committing whatever crime was on her mind now.

It only vaguely occurred to him that he was going to chase her down and stop her, only to drag her back to his place. A reasonable man would just leave her alone, let her fall down and make her mistakes, but something urged him forward, determined to save her, even if it was from herself.

He caught up with her just as she was exiting the building. Instead of announcing his presence and demanding that she march right back upstairs, and into his bed where he could keep an eye on her, he waited, watching to see where she might be going.

When she ducked into the convenience store on the corner, he blinked in surprise. Was she out of cash? Was she going to rob the place? He stood on the stoop, wondering what he should do. A sane lawyer would call the police and have her arrested but everything inside of him rebelled at the idea of Mia being in handcuffs again. No, he couldn't do that to her. Not again. His stomach clenched at the idea of anyone touching her with handcuffs. Well, except himself, he thought with a handful of lusty thoughts.

Shaking his head to clear out those images, he reminded himself that the police wouldn't be gentle if they arrived to arrest her again when it was their second arrest in less than twenty-four hours.

So when she appeared in his line of sight again, her arms loaded down with something he couldn't immediately identify, he went through what he knew of her. She didn't have a gun, at least not one that he could see. So how was she going to rob the store? He knew the store owner and wouldn't allow her to hurt any of Louey's employees. Louey was a good guy with five kids and ten grandkids. He needed every cent he could earn from the convenience store.

He was actually still standing there, debating what to do when the night shift employee laughed at something Mia said to him and started loading whatever she'd dumped onto the counter into a large, brown bag.

Was she stealing supplies for some heist? He saw her hand the guy a credit card and something in his chest eased somewhat. A true criminal wouldn't purchase items with a credit card. It was too easy to trace. Okay, that was yet another ridiculous thought. A true criminal wouldn't even have credit cards. Would they?

So what was she buying? What on earth could be so important that she had to go out in the middle of the night when she should be exhausted after the day she'd had.

When she came out of the store, he was still standing there, glaring down at her with his hands on his hips. "What was so important, Mia?" he asked.

He had a small sense of satisfaction to see her startled reaction to his presence. She looked up at him, worried and trying to hide the bag under her arm. "Ash! What on earth are you doing up at this time of the night?" she demanded.

Ash wasn't going to let her hide anything from him. "Remember what I said earlier today about full disclosure?" he asked, moving closer to her, invading her space before he wrenched the brown paper bag out of her hands. "What did you need that was so urgent that you had to sneak out at…?" He was looking into the bag and words failed him. He blinked once. Then again. Trying to focus on what he was seeing.

Impossible!

"Mia! What the hell were you doing sneaking out in the middle of the night to buy ice cream?" he demanded angrily.

Mia shifted on her feet, feeling embarrassed to be caught with her kryptonite. "Just give it back to me!" she demanded, holding out her hands and trying to get it back from him without actually touching him. She'd thought he looked nice in a suit and then he'd revealed a bit of that tanned, yummy looking skin over dinner. Now he was wearing jeans that molded to his muscular thighs and a tee shirt that was stretched taught over those bulging muscles in his arms and chest. That wasn't fair! He should be ugly or flabby or short and rude or…something! The man was just…damn him! He was hot!

Ash laughed as the relief surged through him. "You couldn't sleep so you had to sneak out and get…" he counted quickly, "six different flavors of ice cream?" he demanded.

"Give me back my bag!" she growled, reaching up and trying to take her ice cream bag back. But he was too tall and he held it over his head, way out of her reach. "You're being a jerk, Ash. Just give me back my bag!"

Ash wrapped his arm around her waist, laughing at her angry expression. "Don't you remember me telling you that everything you need is in my place?" he asked.

She sighed and glared up at him, pressing her palms against his chest, trying to put some room between their bodies, but he wasn't giving an inch and she was starting to react to his closeness. She needed that ice cream! "Ash, if you don't give me back my bag, I'm not going to be responsible for my actions!" She wished she could come up with something more specific, some dire threat that would make him reconsider holding her ice cream away from her. But she couldn't think about anything with his arm around her waist. And he smelled so good! Now that she was closer to him, she could smell his spicy, male scent that filled up her nostrils and made her ache to bury her nose in his chest or against his neck and just…inhale!

"Come with me," he said and grabbed her hand, pulling her back to his building.

"You're being a bully!" she said, following simply because she didn't have a choice. First of all, she wasn't going to be able to sleep until she'd had her ice cream which he didn't seem inclined to give back to her. And secondly, when Ash wanted her to move somewhere, he didn't really take no for an answer.

In the small elevator, she pressed her shoulders back against the paneled wall and crossed her arms over her chest. "You're a rude, insensitive jerk, you know that?"

Even words didn't hurt the big lug, she thought with resentment. He just laughed at her anger. When the front door opened up, he grabbed her hand again and pulled her all the way through to his stainless steel and brick kitchen. When the two of them were standing in front of the enormous freezer, he looked down at her a moment before opening the door.

And Mia just stared, not sure if she could believe her eyes.

Row after row on his freezer sat just about every different kind of ice cream she could imagine. There were maybe twenty different kinds and her mouth started drooling. "You're kidding!" she gasped with delight and surprise.

"I guess I should have told you that I love ice cream," he said. He turned to face her and a moment later, his hands were on her waist lifting her up. He lifted her easily and set her back down on the counter behind her. "My favorite is praline pecan, but feel free to try out each one and give it a try."

Mia thought she might have just died and gone to heaven. When Ash put a spoon in front of her face, she grabbed it, then twisted around, balancing herself on the counter while she grabbed the chocolate brownie ice cream. She didn't say a word but instead, dove into the ice cream, leaning against the counter behind her while she spooned the rich, creamy dessert into her mouth.

"I think I might have to marry you," she mumbled, then realized what she'd just said and looked up at him, startled and worried about his reaction.

He was reaching into the freezer himself and opened up the cherry vanilla ice cream, his own spoon already in his hand. "I accept. When's the wedding?"

Mia's mind froze and she looked up at him, suddenly realizing what she'd just said. When he only winked down at her as he dug into his own ice cream container, she sighed with relief. He was only taking the comment as a joke, which was how it was meant. Sort of.

Her mind froze again. Okay, she asked herself mentally, where had that "sort of" come from? Of course she'd been teasing! She shifted on the counter, tucking her feet underneath her and taking another large spoonful of the chocolate dessert. "Why couldn't you sleep?" she asked

He took a large spoonful of the cherry vanilla, then put the top back on the container and pulled out the rocky road. "I was sound asleep. I heard you sneak out and it woke me up."

She looked up at him sheepishly, feeling horrible for disturbing his slumber. "I'm sorry," she said and took another bite. "Whenever I have trouble sleeping, ice cream always makes me fall asleep faster. Probably the sugar and the milk, or something."

They talked a little about the case, more about their favorite ice creams and some about the different things they did to relax when they were stressed about work or life. By the time she was yawning, it was almost one o'clock in the morning.

"I think I can go to sleep now," she said with a sleepy smile and jumped off of the counter. She put the cartons of mostly melted ice cream back into the freezer, feeling self-conscious now that he was watching her in her bare feet, looking bedraggled after a long, difficult day.

She leaned against the counter slightly, smiling up at him. "Well...." She felt awkward and that painful awareness came raging back. "Good night," she said softly. "Again."

He chuckled, but moved closer, inexorably drawn to her softness. "Goodnight, Mia," he replied.

He wanted to touch her, to kiss her but it was late. She'd been up for almost twenty-four hours and he refused to take advantage of her.

Mia shifted on her feet, feeling a strange sort of power overtake her. It might have just been exhaustion, but she didn't care. Not at this point anyway.

She walked over to him and lifted up on her bare feet. She'd meant to just give him a soft, gentle kiss and then skitter away.

That was the plan anyway.

She lifted up but she lost her balance slightly and reached out to steady herself by placing her hand in the middle of his chest. She looked at her hand, felt his heartbeat underneath her fingers. She just stared, barely moving, barely breathing. For a long moment, they just stood there like that.

She felt her eyes move upwards as if in slow motion. She'd seen this in the movies so many times but it was surreal now. When her eyes looked into his, there was a complete awareness of him as a man.

Her hand moved higher, her fingers wrapping around his neck and she lifted her head to kiss him. She held her breath, needing so desperately to feel his lips against hers, to know what it was like to be kissed by this man. He hesitated for only a fraction of a second before lowering his head. She couldn't have kissed him without his help and she almost sobbed with relief when his lips finally touched hers.

She gasped at the heat that erupted with that barely-there touch. Mia pulled back, startled and looked into his eyes. He was looking right back at her. But his expression hardened, the heat flared to a roaring fire and his hands, which had been gripping the stone counter behind him, whipped around to hold her close, pulling her even more solidly against his hard body. One hand dove into her hair, holding her head in place while his lips ravished hers and the other arm wrapped round her waist, lifting her higher against his hard frame and making her whimper with need.

After that first touch, he wasn't gentle. But nor did Mia want gentleness. She might have cried against any kind of tenderness from this man. Right now, she desperately wanted only to be devoured. She wanted everything this hard, kind, generous and intelligent man had to give and he delivered without further hesitation. Over and over again he tilted his head, kissing her, his tongue diving into her mouth and demanding that hers mate with his. And when she complied, her whole body melted into his as he pulled her even closer.

She didn't feel him lift her up or spin her around. All she knew was that his heat was spreading to every portion of her body. Her mind was no longer in control. Only desire had control. Her hands were gripping his hair, holding him close so he couldn't get away. When he tore his mouth away from hers, she whimpered with need but the hand in her hair pulled her head backwards and she sighed with delight when his mouth nibbled on her neck and her earlobe, causing her to shudder with increased need. And then suddenly his mouth was back, he was demanding more, kissing her as if he were feeling everything she was feeling. She thrilled to that need in him even as it scared her a little.

And then it was over. He pulled back, their breathing heavy as they looked at each other. Realization slowly dawned on her and her mind started working once again. She looked around, getting her bearings. She was no longer standing on the floor but instead, she was sitting on his countertop, his hips between her legs and pressing against her core.

He pulled back just as she realized their position.

"I'm sorry, Mia. That won't happen again," he said softly. With strong, deft fingers, he lifted her off of the counter top. But then he walked stiffly away, taking the stairs two or three at a time as he put as much space between them as he could.

Mia stood there for several more minutes, wondering how a simple kiss had gotten so out of control. She'd never experienced anything like that before. And to experience it now, with a man she didn't even like? And who...

"Oh no," she sighed, the horrifying events of the day surging back to her mind.

"No," she told herself firmly. Shaking her head, she pulled herself together. With equal parts exhaustion and determination, she slowly made her way up the stairs and to the bedroom he'd loaned her. Sliding between the sheets, her last thought was if she would ever be able to fall asleep after that kiss.

Over the next three days, Ash worked like a demon. He was everywhere, arguing with the district attorney, examining evidence, going through all the documents the police had picked up and doing just about everything he could to get the charges dropped.

During the day, he kept Mia close by. Sometimes she would be working with Mark or his team. Other times, he might have her right next to him while his legal team went through the evidence.

The nights were the hardest though. He wouldn't let her go home, coming up with one reason after another why she should stay in his brownstone. He cooked dinner for her every night and talked with her about whatever came to mind while they drank wine or beer. He loved the fact that she enjoyed both.

And every night, he kissed her goodnight, enjoying the soft way she responded to his touch. She never failed to drive him crazy with her touch, but he was also careful not to let things get too out of control. It was hard because his body was aching to possess hers. But there was a line he wouldn't cross and making love to a client, especially one as vulnerable and kind as Mia, was something he simply wouldn't do no matter how much his body hurt.

CHAPTER 5

Ash gripped his cell phone in his hand, worry surpassing all other emotions right now. "Mia, where are you?" he demanded, knowing she'd left his place and she wasn't here in the office with him. That meant she wasn't where he could protect her and he didn't like that feeling.

He'd left his brownstone this morning after checking on her, watching her sleep for perhaps a bit longer than might be appropriate. But after their kiss last night, he'd had trouble tearing his eyes away from her. She'd looked so peaceful this morning – the exact opposite of how he felt right now.

"I'm just heading over to my place. I need some different clothes and I need to figure out what's going on with my house. I'm a little anxious after you mentioned the relatively fresh cement in my basement that was being torn up. It was put into the basement to stop the recurring flooding so now there's the added possibility that my house might flood with the next heavy rain."

Since Ash had just discussed the status of her little cottage with the police detective in charge of the investigation, his stomach clenched with worry over her reaction to what her house might look like. "Mia, if you need something, have Autumn go over and get it. If she's unavailable, I'll get someone else to do it or I'll do it myself," he said, quickly grabbing his coat off of the back of his chair and rushing out of the office. He might have known Mia for a little only a few days, but he was already starting to get to know this stubborn little woman and he was pretty sure she would ignore his suggestion.

She laughed and he gritted his teeth. She was certainly in a wonderful mood this morning. It was amazing what a good night's sleep had done for her. He wished he could say the same. That kiss had driven all possibility of sleep out of his mind last night. He'd lain awake, thinking of her soft, warm body in the bed just one room next to him and he'd ached to touch her again, hear her soft sighs when he touched her silky skin.

"Ash, don't worry about me. I'm tired of relying on everyone else, especially when I'm perfectly able to do things for myself."

Ash pressed the call button for the elevator several times, frantic to get to her before she saw what the police had done to her house. "Mia, just turn around and head back to my place," he said with what he hoped was a gentle voice but he wasn't sure. He was gritting his teeth as he spoke, too worried about her seeing her yard. "No one thinks you're relying on them too much. We're more than happy to help."

"I'm fine, Ash. Thank you for your help, but I'm just going to run home, take a shower with my own stuff and get my own clothes. I know the press might still be a problem so I'll be careful."

She wasn't listening to him and everything she said made perfect sense, but he knew the details! He had to stop her somehow! "Mia, don't you dare go back to your house," he commanded, relying on old instincts.

Mia pulled the cell phone back from her ear. "What just happened here?" she asked, her voice definitely colder. "You can't order me about, Ash."

He knew that was the truth but he didn't like it. Hell, he wished he had the right to simply tell her to turn around, or even better, he wished she trusted him enough to listen to him and trust him. That didn't make any difference now. She would be so upset if she saw her house. He just knew it!

"Mia, after the past few nights, I can damn well tell you what to do and I want you to tell the cab driver to turn around and head back to my place or to my office right now. If you don't want anyone else in your place, fine. I'll get your stuff for you later. Or even better, I'll bring you there myself." Really, he just didn't want her to see what had happened before he could fix everything. "Just turn around now," he said with as much authority as he could muster under the circumstances. "I'm getting in the elevator now. I'll meet you back at my place."

Mia was irritated with his tone and wasn't going to take orders from him or any man. Not after everything that had happened over the past week. "Goodbye Ash," she said and pressed the end button on her cell phone.

She dumped it right back into her purse, then fished it out again and pressed the silent mode. If she knew anything about Ash by now, it was that he didn't give up. He'd call her right back.

Ash stared at his phone for half a second before his anger exploded. He immediately hit redial even while he was rushing to his car. When her voice mail picked up, he was furious and worried all at the same time. "Damn it, Mia. Pick up the phone and call me back. Don't you dare go over to your house! I'm telling you now to just turn around. I'll take you over there myself tonight."

He dove into his car, tires screeching as he pulled out of the parking space. He ran three red lights in an attempt to get to her place faster. He didn't want her seeing what the police had done. After everything she'd gone through, this would be the final blow. He didn't know what she would do and he didn't want to take the chance that this would be the straw that broke her.

He pressed the call button on his steering wheel, cursing when he got her voice mail again. "Mia, call me back right now! I'm ordering you to stop doing this and call me!"

He drove three more miles and pressed the button again. When he only got her voice mail one more time, he shook his head and pressed the accelerator. "Mia, don't do this. I'm telling you," he said, changing from anger to coaxing, determined to stop her somehow, "just turn around and come back to my place."

She didn't even look at her cell phone again, feeling empowered now that she was finally heading home. She felt like she'd been gone for months instead of just days and she was eager to be around her own things, to sort through her mind and figure out what was going on.

Mia already had the money ready to pay the cab driver before they turned the corner on her street. But when the cab driver pulled up in front of her house, she couldn't believe her eyes. With a horrible, stabbing pain shooting through her entire body, she handed the cab driver the money and stepped out of the vehicle. Unfortunately, she couldn't go any further.

Her entire front yard was torn up. All her carefully planted hydrangeas, which had been lovely earlier in the summer, some pink, some blue and some with a creamy white, were just a wilted, scattered mess on the ground. Her roses and hostas, all were reduced to clumps of brown on top of the sidewalk. Even her grass had been torn up. There wasn't anything that wasn't destroyed. She could even see through her back gate that the backyard was worse than the front, if that was even possible.

She'd spent so many happy hours working on her garden, researching the plants that would grow easily in this area, making sure that they were well fertilized with organic compost, going around to the various coffee shops and getting extra coffee grounds, asking all of her neighbors to save their egg shells and banana peels just so her hostas were a deep, dark green and her roses could make it through the harsh winters and tough summers. And now everything was destroyed! It wasn't just that the yard had been dug up, it had been destroyed. She had no idea how to save these plants. If holes had been dug around them, she could help the plants survive. But these guys had been out of the soil for several days now. They hadn't had any water or food and their roots had dried up from the heat and no protection.

She just stood there, her heart breaking as the pain of her little house sunk in.

She didn't even hear the car skid to a halt behind her. But she felt Ash's presence as soon as he was next to her. She could feel his heat and that odd sense of security and sexual tension that she always felt when he was around her.

"Mia…" he started to say, not sure how to explain the disaster her home had become. He wasn't even looking at the house, only at her devastated expression and he ached to fix it somehow for her.

She didn't say anything, just looked up into his eyes. A moment later, she threw herself towards him and Ash closed his arms around her, holding her close and whispering in her ear how sorry he was for what the investigators had done to her house. It was the worst he'd ever seen. Never in his career had any search warrant gone this far but he suppressed his anger in order to help Mia through this devastation.

Mia had no idea how long she cried but when the sobbing slowed to an ebb, she remained in Ash's arms, drawing strength from him. With him holding her like this, she knew she could get through just about anything.

She pulled back slightly, noticing the wet area on his chest where her tears had dampened his shirt. He looked down at her, the kindness and anger obvious in his eyes. That anger was on her behalf and not directed at her and even that made her feel better, comforted somehow. "Come on, Mia. Let me get you out of here. I'm sorry you had to see this," he said gently.

Mia smiled up at him. "Is that why you were trying to order me around earlier?"

He chuckled softly despite his frustration over her stubbornness. "Yes. I knew what they'd done."

She felt better now. So he wasn't just trying to be a jerk. He was trying to be a sweet, kind man. "Thank you," she replied sincerely, taking a deep breath and turning back to her cottage. "Well, I guess I have a lot of work to do." She put her hands on her hips and looked around, mentally taking an inventory of all that needed to be done.

"I guess it's probably worse inside, isn't it?" she asked, not bothering to turn around and look up at him. She knew the answer. If they'd thought she'd buried him and torn up the yard, she suspected that they might have even considered that she'd chopped up the body and hid it inside her walls somehow. That was a gruesome thought so she pushed it aside, deciding not to borrow trouble until she knew the extent of the interior damage. Don't borrow trouble, she told herself firmly.

She walked up the path, bending down to examine some of the plants that were littered along the way. "They could have been a bit kinder on the roots," she said, almost to herself.

Ash walked behind her, not exactly sure what to do or how to help her through this. He was also confused as to what might be going through her mind. Only moments ago, she'd been sobbing out her anguish over her devastated home and now she was walking through the war-like zone as if this were just another chore.

"Mia?" he called out, reaching down to touch her shoulder.

Mia stood, looking up at him with a wilted hosta plant in each hand. "What's wrong?" she asked.

Ash didn't know what to say. "What's wrong?" he repeated, stunned that she would even ask. "Your house is destroyed, your plants all killed and you're still facing murder charges. That's what's wrong." He put his hands on her shoulders, trying to determine how upset she really was. If he were in her shoes, he'd be furious and launching a full out law suit against the city for the way they'd handled this search warrant.

Mia sighed, glanced around one more time, then smiled up at him. "Yes, that's all true. I can't do anything about the murder charges. I have to leave that up to you and just answer any questions that come up. You're the brilliant lawyer who has kept me out of jail so you're on top of that, as far as I'm concerned." She sighed as she continued. "I can't figure out what happened to Jeff. Something inside of me is telling me that he's fine, possibly on a warm, lush Caribbean island somewhere hanging out, not even aware that people are looking for him, but I can't believe that even he is that self-centered. Besides, I don't have my passport, so it isn't like I can fly off and search for him, can I?" She looked around at her yard, determination brightening her cheeks and stiffening her spine. "But I can do something about my yard. And you're going to get rid of the murder charges for me. Everything else is just noise."

It struck him how sensible her attitude was. And yes, he was definitely going to get her out of these ridiculous murder charges. The district attorney's office couldn't even find the body, but that didn't eliminate the possibility of a conviction, it just made it harder for the prosecution to prove their case. But circumstantial evidence could prove the case for them. It was dangerous to rely on reasonable thinking in these kinds of situations. Not everyone on a jury was reasonable.

"Mark and the rest of my team are slowly breaking down the prosecution's case, Mia. We'll get rid of these charges and figure out what really happened." He looked around the yard again, "But you can't stay here. Come on back to my place and I'll get someone out here to fix this for you."

Mia shook her head. "Goodness, I can't afford anyone to come clean up this mess for me," she replied.

After everything else, he couldn't let her deal with this. It was just too much. "Let me do this for you," he countered, determined to protect her however possible.

She smiled, grateful for the offer but shook her head. "I can't let you do that. You already feel bad enough." She sighed and looked around. "Besides, I enjoy gardening." She grimaced slightly and looked up at him. "Just make sure my freezer is stocked with ice cream tonight because I'm going to be pretty sore."

Ash wanted to curse but refrained, knowing that it would offend Mia. "I want to do this," he argued. "And you don't need this extra burden."

"Actually," she smiled and looked around, "fixing up all of this will give me something to do rather than worry about Jeff and the upcoming trial. I don't mind the work. Since I can't go to school until this is figured out, I might as well do something productive." She smiled up at him. "It will be just like your house renovations. You mentioned how easy it was to work through problems while you're working with wood or staining something. Well, I feel the same way about gardening. It makes me feel strong and powerful, somehow giving back to the earth a little bit." She shrugged her shoulders as she said, "Gardening is good for the soul."

Out of the corner of his eye, Ash caught a movement coming down the sidewalk. His first instinct was to shove her back into his car, not wanting her to have to deal with whatever some mean-spirited neighbor wanted to say to her.

They both turned at the same time to find an elderly couple approaching. Ash was just about to push Mia behind him, protecting her from what he expected would be a brutal verbal assault. Neighbors usually trusted the police, so when they arrested someone, the community automatically assumed that the person was guilty.

Ash was again stunned. The couple stopped right in front of her, their eyes gentle and concerned without even a hint of malice. "Mia, tell us where we can help," the man who looked to be about sixty or sixty-five, said while his wife nodded next to him. "We're here to fix up all this mess and get you back on your feet."

The woman reached out and gently touched Mia's hand, showing her support with the tender touch. "We couldn't believe what the police did to your beautiful yard, dear. We told them over and over again that you didn't kill that horrible man. We know you didn't do it. So just tell us what you need and we're here for you, honey."

Mia smiled warmly to the couple, reaching out to shake their hands. Instead, the couple reached out and gave her a bone crushing hug. "That's so generous of you," she said and Ash could hear the wobble in her tone again.

When she pulled back, she introduced Ash to the couple. "Arnie, Beth, this is my attorney, Ash Thorpe. Ash, these are the Corrinders. They live about three houses down and have four kids and ten grandkids."

Arnie Corrinder squinted at Ash and came a bit closer. "You're going to get our girl out of this mess, right? There's absolutely no way she could have murdered that slime, but if he ever turns up, you'd better believe I'm going to kill him for what he's put our girl through!"

Ash was so surprised that the man was confessing to murderous thoughts that he grinned. "I have a whole team of people who are working long hours to figure out who actually killed Mr. Meyers."

Beth shook her head. "I can't believe Jeff just disappeared, but I really don't like that new fiancée of his," she explained, latching onto Mia's arm protectively. "I'm sure she's up to something. When Jeff finally turns up, dead or alive, I'm putting my money on him being in her basement somehow." The woman tsked, shaking her head before she said, "Probably chained up and gagged just to keep his mouth shut," she said to her husband with a completely serious expression. "He tried to kick the Jameson's dog," she said as if that explained everything. "And when the Jameson's stopped him, that stupid man actually yelled at them. As if he had every right to stand out here and wake us up on a Saturday morning with his ridiculous wrath."

Mia nodded, remembering that day. "That was one of the times he'd shown up, unannounced, trying to get me to reconsider our engagement. It happened about two months ago."

Ash heard something behind him and spun around. There were about five more people coming from different directions, some had shovels and other gardening tools in their hands and all of them looked ready to either attack Mia as a mob or attack the dirt, he wasn't sure which.

"We saw ya coming!" one man said as he rounded the corner, pushing a wheelbarrow filled with gardening tools. "We're here to help! Just tell us what you need."

Mia's eyes turned misty and she bowed her head. Ash thought he might have spied her shoulders shake slightly, but she shook it off and lifted her head. He almost gasped at the glow of happiness that surrounded her at that moment. He was stunned by the beauty both inside of her and around her as her friends and neighbors surrounded her, dropping what they were doing so they could show up and help replant her devastated yard.

"They tore up the inside, too, Mia. Don't you dare go inside," a female voice said. Ash turned around and there were five women, all who had buckets, brooms and mops. "You just give us your house key and stay out here to direct the work. We'll be inside, cleaning up what those bastards did to your house."

Ash shook his head, never having witnessed anything so astonishing. One and all just took a corner of the yard and started raking or digging, ready to try and plant the wilted shrubs and rose bushes. One man even swore he could revive the hostas and piled all of them up into his arms as if they were his babies.

By the end of the day, the yard was back in order. He suspected it wasn't up to its previous glory, but it looked pretty good. He'd secretly called a gardening center and had several new bushes delivered. He had no idea what to order, but told them to bring stuff that was hardy as well as a load of mulch. He also ordered fifty pizzas to be delivered. The pizzas arrived at noon and someone brought out pitchers of lemonade and even some beer. No one stopped working though. The gardening center's truck pulled up after the pizza had been devoured and everyone simply took a bush or a bag of mulch and planted the bush, surrounding the roots with the mulch for protection from the upcoming winter. The nights were already cooler with cold starting to seep into the air. The fall was a strange time when one day could be hot, everyone walking around in short sleeves, while the next one everyone needed a coat.

No matter how many times her neighbors told her to stand back, Mia was right there in the thick of the repairs. She was covered in sweat and dirt, smiling at anyone who approached her to ask her where she wanted one plant or another. Even Ash drove home and changed into jeans and a tee-shirt. It took him less than an hour, but he was right back there, doing all the heavy lifting so the elderly people wouldn't hurt themselves. Anything that had to be moved or lifted, he tried to insert himself. Several times throughout the day, he looked over at her and winked or just absorbed her happiness. There wasn't much he could do, but the more he looked at her, the more he wanted her in his bed. He wanted to be the one to give her that contentment or excited expression.

If she would just stop this assertion that he was only trying to comfort her, they could curl up together, just the two of them tonight, and find bliss in each other's arms. And if he could just get this murder charge out of the way, he could show her how much he was starting to care for her. In just a few days, she'd gotten under his skin like no other woman ever had.

By the end of the day, just as the sun was setting over the horizon, he stood next to her as the last of her neighbors gave her a weak hug and walked down the sidewalk to their own homes. Every single one of them told him to call if he needed anything to get her out of this mess.

When the door closed on the last one, Mia looked across the room at Ash. "You stink," she teased.

Ash laughed and moved forward. "And you look sexy as hell," he replied. He'd enjoyed working with her today, laughing with her, watching her with her neighbors. She treated each of them as if they were special and, in turn, they treated her as if she were one of their children.

Mia rolled her eyes. "I probably smell worse than you."

"Where's your shower?" he asked.

Her eyes widened. "Shower?"

"Yes, the place where water comes down out of a faucet and there's generally soap?" He didn't wait for her to answer. Instead, he walked up the stairs to find it himself. "Never mind," he called back down the stairs. Then slammed the bathroom door closed.

She heard the water turn on and her mind couldn't stop picturing him in the shower. And she had an extremely good imagination. The hot water running down those muscles would be like a work of art, she thought. She could just imagine taking her washcloth and smoothing soap all over his chest, those powerful arms and all of that delicious skin on his back. On second thought, forget the washcloth. She wanted her hands on him. She didn't want anything between her fingers and his skin.

In less time than she would have liked, the water shut off again. It took him only moments before the door opened. He moved down the stairs, one hand holding a pink towel over his head as he rubbed his hair and another pink towel precariously wrapped around his lean hips. The towel was perfectly sized for her, but on him, the material barely went around his muscular legs, giving her an eyeful whenever he took a step.

She knew she was staring, but as he approached, she didn't think any woman in the world would blame her. The man was…shocking! Every part of his body was covered with muscles. She suspected that his body fat percentage was somewhere in the zero range. There wasn't a single part of the man that wasn't perfectly chiseled.

He was standing over her, looking down at her before he said, "Your turn," with that sexy, no-nonsense voice of his.

Mia wasn't sure what he was talking about. "My turn?" she asked, wondering if she was going to get her turn at touching all that wonderful, delicious, incredible…

"For a shower," he clarified.

Mia was stumped. A shower had been so far from her mind that it didn't even make sense. And then it struck her. "Shower!" she exclaimed and stood upright. "Yes, a shower!"

She stepped around him, moving up the stairs as quickly as possible. She was proud of herself for only stumbling on three of the steps but figured she earned extra credit for not turning around and gawking at him some more.

In the shower, she leaned against the door, smelling her own soap mingled with the maleness that was pure "Ash".

"You're in deep," she whispered to herself.

"Hurry up, Mia. I'll make some dinner."

That startled her away from the door and she reached in to turn on the shower. She didn't see where his clothes were, but she stripped off her own and threw them into the hamper. She stepped into the warm water, feeling a strong sense of intimacy, knowing that Ash had been in here only a few minutes ago. She loved how it felt to have the bathroom already warm from the steam of his shower.

She was so lost in the fantasy in her mind where Ash was still in the shower and he was helping her wash off…and she got to help him wash off, she didn't hear the knock on the door.

It wasn't until he poked his face behind the shower curtain that she realized he was in her bathroom and she yelped, trying to hide her nakedness with whatever she had. And the plastic scrunchie filled with soap really wasn't up to the task. His smile, and the dark glance down her body, told her that she was failing completely.

"You're too slow, babe. Hurry up. Dinner is ready."

With that, his face disappeared again and she heard the door close softly.

It still took her several minutes before she was able to move again. But after that, she rushed through her shower in record time, rinsing out the shampoo and conditioner faster than she thought possible.

In her bedroom, she tightened the towel around her chest, staring at her closet, trying to figure out what to wear.

"What's taking so long?" he asked, standing right behind her.

Mia spun around, her fingers once more grabbing the towel that was knotted just under her arms. "What are you doing in here?" she gasped. She looked him up and down, painfully disappointed that he'd lost the pink towel and was now wearing a clean pair of jeans and yet another one of those tee-shirts that made her drool as she took in the muscles straining the fabric to the limit.

"Trying to figure out why you're letting our dinner get cold." His eyes traveled up and down her damp figure with appreciation. "If you're trying to figure out if that works for you, let me be the first to say that I am in full agreement with you coming down exactly like that," he said with a sexy leer on his handsome face.

She grabbed a pair of yoga pants from her closet and a clean tee-shirt. "I'll be down in less than five minutes," she promised.

"Make it two," he told her, then disappeared again.

Mia didn't challenge him. She pulled on the yoga pants, a bra and tee shirt, then added a pair of socks, as if they could protect her against what she was feeling right now. Socks really weren't the best protection against throwing herself into Ash's arms, but she didn't have much else. Her thinking was, if she looked homely enough, it would keep her from wanting him as much.

As soon as she walked down the stairs, she knew that her thinking was painfully flawed. His hot eyes looked up from the plates that he'd already set up on the counter. Those eyes traveled from the top of her head where her hair was still wet, all the way down her body to her sock-clad toes peeking out from underneath her yoga pants.

"Is that what you wear to yoga class?" he asked, gripping the spatula in one hand and the handle of the pan in the other.

"Yes," she replied, smoothing her hands down her thighs self-consciously.

He nodded slowly, his eyes still moving along her petite figure. "I might just take up yoga so I can watch one day."

The idea of this big, strong, masculine man attending her yoga class, moving into all the various positions, somehow seemed hilariously funny to her. "I don't think that would be a good idea," she replied. "What did you make for dinner this time?" she asked, walking up to the counter and looking down at the plates.

"Pancakes. You need to get food other than diet meals," he growled and looked down, piling two more pancakes on her plate. "And what's with this veggie sausage?" he asked with obvious distrust. "I don't think anything that isn't meat should try and pass itself off as meat." But he plunked three of them on his plate and two on hers.

She laughed again, relieved by the slight dispersion in the sexual tension between them. "The sausages are delicious," she replied, shaking her head because she usually had only one of them for breakfast with a piece of fruit. She'd never be able to eat all that food, but Ash couldn't seem to grasp that she ate about a third of what he could go through during a meal.

"And you need real syrup," he snarled, plunking the sugar free syrup onto the middle of the table. "Sit," he said but softened the order by pulling out her chair, then sliding it in when she was seated. He then moved to the chair opposite her and she couldn't help but smile at how sexy he looked in her periwinkle kitchen surrounded by shabby chic curtains and pillows, not to mention the flowers on the window sill looking out from over her sink. The police hadn't done any permanent damage and even her inside plants and flowers were saved from their ruthless search, probably because they knew she couldn't hide a body in their small pots.

"What's so funny?" he asked as he cut up his enormous stack of pancakes, then poured her sugar-free syrup all over them.

"You."

He looked up, his dark eyebrows raised in question.

She couldn't help but laugh. He was just so tough looking – the complete antithesis of her entire household décor. "You just don't fit in with the pretty periwinkle kitchen," she said, laughing once again.

He rolled his eyes. "I should probably take offense at that, but I can't help but agree. My masculinity is at risk here."

She giggled but stuffed a bite of pancakes into her mouth, savoring the amazing taste. "What did you put into these?" she asked, closing her eyes in surprise.

"Vanilla and cinnamon," he came back, pouring her a glass of milk. "You need beer, too."

She sighed as if she were in heaven. "I have lemonade if you don't like milk."

He shook his head as if that were completely out of the question. "You're too wholesome. I need to do something about that."

Mia cringed. "Not totally wholesome," she said under her breath, thinking of her thoughts as he came out of the bathroom.

She was looking down at her plate when she said that but her eyes snapped up when she heard his knife and fork clatter onto the plate. "What do you mean by that?" he demanded, his eyes staring into hers with an intensity that caused all rational thinking to fly out the window.

"Um…I…just…"

"What unwholesome thoughts are you thinking, Mia?" he asked. His tone was soft, but it definitely wasn't gentle. Coaxing was a better term to describe the way he was speaking to her. As if he wanted her to reveal….

"I just…" she shrugged, blushing painfully and unable to maintain eye contact with him.

"Might you be having unwholesome thoughts about me?" he asked.

Mia looked up, startled that he could read her so easily. But then again, what else was he supposed to think. "I…"

He could see that she was embarrassed. But he could also see the truth in her eyes. "I can guarantee that almost none of my thoughts are very wholesome when you're around."

With that, her whole body heated up in flash so intense, she thought her chair might catch on fire. In fact, she wiggled slightly, uncomfortable now that she was on one side of the table and he was on the other. "You're my lawyer."

"I am. But I won't be soon."

"Because I'll be in jail?" she gasped.

"No. Because you'll be free. And you won't be my client any longer."

She fiddled with her fork, not sure what to do with her hands when she desperately wanted to run them over those shoulders like she had the last time he'd kissed her. "You're that far ahead on the case?" she asked, hoping that he would confirm that. She didn't even think about her being free. She just wanted him to want her, to believe in her innocence.

"I spoke to the prosecutor this morning before you decided to head over here to investigate. We discussed your case and every time he brought up an issue, I was able to slap it down. He doesn't have much to go on now. And he knows it."

Mia breathed a sigh of relief. "So the charges are going to be dropped, right?"

"I can't guarantee anything," he cautioned.

She smiled slightly, knowing deep down inside that he believed in her. That he knew she hadn't done this horrible thing they were accusing her of. "So that's it? It will all be over?"

"Don't get too excited," he said and leaned over to hold her hand. "I don't want you to get your hopes up about anything because I don't know what will happen tomorrow."

She looked down at his dark fingers tangling with her paler ones, her eyes entranced by the image. What would it be like to have more than her fingers tangled with more than his? What would it be like to have him kiss her and not stop? She'd never wanted this from any other man and she wanted this from him so desperately.

No more fears, she told herself firmly. So when his fingers tightened around hers, she went willingly into his arms, feeling his strong body against hers and reveling in the magic of his touch.

"What about dinner?" she asked, uncaring herself what happened to the food as long as she could continue to feel him touching her like this.

"That's not dinner," he groaned as he lifted her into his arms. "That's unreal sausage and unreal syrup."

She couldn't stop the laughter, but it quickly died when his mouth covered hers. A moment later, he lifted her into his arms and carried her back up the stairs, laying her gently on the bed. "Are you sure about this Mia?" he asked carefully, leaning over her but holding his weight away from hers.

Mia writhed under him, almost angry that he was holding his body away from hers. "I'm very sure," she gasped out. That was the last time she had a moment to talk. He didn't wait for her to change her mind or realize that this wasn't a good idea. If he were a better man, he would hold back until her name was cleared. But he couldn't and he wasn't. He wanted her and it felt like he'd wanted her for so long.

With gentle fingers, he lifted her tee-shirt up and over her head then took a moment to stare down at her soft, full breasts that were almost spilling out of her white, lace bra. "Not too wholesome here," he said with a gravelly voice while his fingers traced the line of her bra, just at the edge, teasing her ever so carefully.

"Ash!" she cried out when he didn't stop or move closer to where she wanted his fingers. "Please!" she gasped. And then he moved closer. Right where she wanted his fingers to be. When his thumb rubbed against the hard nubbin of her nipple, she jerked in reaction and pulled his hand away. But as soon as the sensation was gone, she needed it back again. With her hand holding his wrist, she brought his hand back to her breast, her hand forcing his to cover the whole area.

"Mia!" he groaned and then his head bent, his mouth covering hers while his fingers blindly explored her breast again. First one, then the other, his fingers and palms learned the way she liked to be touched. It seemed that there wasn't any wrong way to touch her, she was so responsive that it made him nearly mad with lust while her body pressed against his hand, her mouth becoming more ravenous as he discovered more secrets about those magnificent globes.

"No more," she gasped when his fingers moved again and she arched against him, almost whimpering with her need and the crazy way he made her feel.

"Much more," he countered and moved his mouth from hers, kissing along her neck, her shoulder and then hovering for a moment over her breast. He waited, wondering what she would do and he almost smiled when she froze, her whole body rigid as she waited for his mouth.

When he took her nipple in his mouth, she practically pushed him off of her but he was prepared for that, remembering her hand pulling his fingers away earlier. So when she tried to grab his head, he simply took her hands in his and had his wicked way with her, holding her still with his body. He didn't stop until she was arching against him once again and then he only stopped so he could move to the other breast, giving it equal attention.

"Ash!" she cried out, desperate for him to stop but not sure if she might be begging him to keep on going either. She wasn't sure about anything right now.

"I know," he said soothingly, but he didn't feel very soothed at all. Her reactions were making him even more crazy. He wanted to just bury himself inside of her heat. Instead, he moved his mouth lower, kissing her along her soft stomach.

Either she was stronger than she appeared or he was in a weak state, because she suddenly lifted up, pushing him backwards. He looked down at her, noting the dreamy look in her eyes and he smiled. Taking off his shirt, he ripped something but didn't look down. "You're mine," he growled as he tossed his jeans behind him. When he was fully naked, he moved closer to her, seeing the worry in her eyes as she took in his size. "It's okay," he crooned, knowing that this would be her first time. He grabbed the foil packet he'd been keeping in his wallet ever since the night of her ice cream adventure. Once he was fully sheathed, he moved down to cover her once again.

"Ash?" she gasped, feeling him against her leg.

"Don't worry," he told her and bent lower, catching her lips with his. Ever so carefully, he kissed her, bringing her back to that heated place where she was moving underneath him, her hips shifting frantically. He suspected she didn't know what she wanted, but he did. When he moved between her legs, he slid one finger inside of her. When she bowed her back, her legs instinctively moving wider for him, he knew she was right back with him.

He felt her slick heat and had to close his eyes to control himself. Every cell in his body wanted to just push into this heat but he wanted her to be with him every step of the way.

When she grabbed his wrist again, he smiled but it might have been more of a grimace. He wasn't sure at this point. "That didn't stop me last time," he said and bent to kiss her stomach, "and it isn't going to stop me this time either."

She quickly started shaking her head, but he didn't give her a chance to argue. He simply slipped another finger inside of her and her grip on his wrist when limp as her body experienced the next level. When her hips shifted, lifting to take his fingers deeper, he couldn't stop himself any longer. Moving over her, he quickly shifted his body into place and switched his fingers for his hard length, entering her hot core slowly so he wouldn't hurt her.

Mia grabbed onto his shoulders, her body no longer under her own control. She wanted this so desperately that she couldn't even form words. She wanted him deeper, but she also wanted him to stop and move away. If he did that though, she might just melt into a pool of desire and then evaporate with the heat.

"Please, now!" she gasped when she felt him move inside her, slightly deeper with each thrust. He was so slow, so gentle and she really didn't want that right now. She wasn't sure how to tell him so she slid her hands down his body. Tomorrow she might be embarrassed about grabbing his butt and pulling him inside her, but at that moment, when he was fully deep inside her, she couldn't be sorry. There was a slight bit of pain, but as she moved her hips, she became fully adjusted to his size and girth. And it felt so perfectly right!

Unfortunately, he started moving and the rightness no longer was present. It wasn't wrong, but could only be described as frantic. When he pulled out, she bit her lip and raised her hips to try and stop him. When he pushed inside her, ever so slowly, she thought she might just scream out or hit him. "Faster!" she cried, not sure what he would do but just instinctively knowing that she needed him to move inside of her, and not at this slow pace.

Ash laughed softly, thrilled that she was so demanding. It was such a turn-on, not to mention feeling her wrap her body around him so perfectly. He lifted her legs, wrapping each one around his waist so he could move deeper and he gave the little lady exactly what she wanted.

As he thrust back and forth, he watched her and could barely hold himself back because Mia in the throes of passion was sensuality personified. She closed her eyes, lifted her hips, her hands moving along his chest and scratching his arms when he moved at a particularly good angle.

In a shorter time than he would have liked, she exploded around him, her body climaxing in such a powerful, mind blowing manner that he almost stopped moving so he could watch her fall apart in his arms. But then his body realized what his mind was about to do and protested vehemently. He pounded into her after that, needing his own release. And when it came, he thought he was actually pouring his life into her slender, beautiful body. It was so complete, so intense that he couldn't even move for a long time afterwards.

Later that night, Ash stared up at the ceiling, holding Mia close against his side. He couldn't believe he had violated his personal code of ethics by sleeping with his client. It was a huge conflict, but as he listened to her deep, even breathing and felt her body snuggle closer to his side, he knew that he wouldn't have changed last night for anything.

He should at least feel guilty, he told himself. But as he examined his feelings, there was absolutely no guilt at all. If he had the chance, he would probably do it all over again. In fact, he would give her a few hours of sleep, and then he would do it all over again. Slowly, more thoroughly. And he would enjoy every single moment of the activity.

So there was really nothing else he could do except make sure that she was proven innocent. As he lay there in her bed surrounded by flowered sheets and flowered pillows, his mind went over every detail of her case. Something was missing besides the victim. He checked off every detail, went through various precedents that could be brought to the issues, ideas that could dismiss the evidence or refute each item when it was brought to court.

When he mentally had everything in place, knowing exactly how he could obliterate the prosecution's case even before it came to trial, he nodded his head. It wasn't good enough though. His ideas would only keep her out of court. They wouldn't prove that she hadn't murdered her ex-fiancé. He had to work harder, find that part that was missing, and bring it to light. He knew it was out there, he just wasn't sure exactly where to look to find it.

But he would.

With a nod of determination, he rolled over and nibbled on Mia's neck. He'd resisted her delectable body while working through everything, but he was finished with his mental checklist and he couldn't resist any longer. She was just too soft, too sweet and just too tempting. His hand smoothed down her body, slowly waking her up and he smiled with anticipation when he saw her smiling even before she opened   her   eyes.

CHAPTER 6

Ash walked into Mia's school building and looked around. He noted a very well-tended school with the children all laughing as they made their orderly way to their classes. The teachers chatted amongst themselves as they herded their pupils from one place to another, all keeping a watchful eye on the students. When the first bell rang, Ash couldn't help but be impressed by how quickly everything and everyone calmed down and moved to their assigned areas. Classroom doors were shut, the halls quieted down and there was an almost tangible feeling of energy everywhere.

He walked into the office and introduced himself. "I'm Ash Thorpe," he said, handing his card to the secretary.

"Oh, goodness!" she gasped and stood up after reading his card. She blushed as she took in his height, but Ash was used to that reaction. "You're the man defending our Mia, aren't you?" she gushed, clasping her hands together with excitement. "We're all thrilled that you've taken her case."

The others in the room all stopped their work and turned to see what was happening, their fingers halted in midair and papers stopped shuffling. He looked around, startled to have received such a reaction. Most of the time, people were wary of lawyers but this group only looked hopeful and eager. Excited?

Ash cleared his throat, his eyes taking in all the details. "I am. I was wondering if I could interview some of the staff. I know that some of Ms. Paulson's co-workers knew Jeff Richardson and might be able to give me some insight."

The other women looked at each other as if sending a silent message. Then they quickly gathered round, even the principal who came out of her office when she overheard the conversation, a very stern looking woman with a severe suit and no-nonsense attitude. All the women hurried to form a loose circle around him, more than eager to help him with any information. "Whatever you need," the principal replied with a nod of her head, her lips compressed as if she thought that were the only expression appropriate for this situation. "We need her back here as soon as possible."

That was news to him. Mia had stayed away from work for the past several days, always available to his team which was great, but he was now confused. "You mean you didn't put her on administrative leave?" he asked, trying to clarify the situation.

The principal waved her hand at her. "Goodness no, but I suppose the school board might have if she hadn't told me that she would need some personal time to sort this out. She's so sweet to be thinking about us at a time like this," the principal said, shaking her head grimly. "I'm Jeanie," she said, extending her hand. "And you just tell us who you need to speak with and we'll rotate that person out of their classroom for however long you need."

Ash couldn't believe this kind of reception. Normally, he had to threaten legal action to get people to take some time out of their day to help him with his work. That was one of the reasons he normally allowed Mark and his team to do these sorts of interviews and report back to him. Why he was here, Ash hadn't really figured out yet.

He mentally shook his head. That wasn't true at all, he accepted. He was here because he was determined to clear Mia's name. He'd made that decision last night while holding her in his arms and he wanted to be personally involved, to see the reactions of her co-workers and hear from others about Jeff and his relationship with Mia, the woman he now considered his.

Taking a piece of paper out of a file folder, he handed it to the principal. "Here's a list of the people Mia said knew of her relationship between Jeff and herself, and had met Jeff or socialized with them," he said, pulling out a neatly typed list of people.

The principal quickly scanned through the list and it was as if the entire office staff went into full-battle mode. "Eleanor," the principal said, handing the list to the secretary, "make a copy of this list and distribute it around to the other teachers. See if anyone is missing from the list that Mr. Thorpe might need to talk to." She turned to another woman. "Jane, could you get the first three people on this list down to the office? It's going to cause some disruption, but everyone will manage."

Two men walked into the office, obviously both staff members themselves. "I just heard that you need people to cover the classrooms to help Mia," they said. "Where do we go first?"

Within ten minutes, Ash was sitting in a conference room with three people, all of whom were telling him wonderful things about Mia and reviling her ex-fiancé. Apparently, no one liked Jeff Richardson and all were furious with him for the way he stalked her after their breakup. They gave him story after story about how Mia would slip out the back door of the school or a side door, parked her car on a side street or rode the bus, anything possible to slip by Jeff's notice so she could come and go from the school without his harassment. It had gotten so bad, one teacher talked about how she'd spoken to a police officer and asked how to get a restraining order.

"Did you follow through?" Ash asked, sitting up, his pen hovering over the notepaper.

The teacher shook her head, her eyes sad with regret. "Unfortunately, I only got the information last week and I was out sick with the flu. So I never got the chance to tell her what to do before all this happened last week. But I'm sure this is just another trick of Jeff's to get her back. He was a conniving snake," she said, anger brimming within her hazel eyes.

Ash left the school several hours later, chuckling at how protective all of the teachers were of Mia. She seemed to draw that out in several people. Including himself, he thought.

The little woman could take care of herself though. He thought of all the times he'd wanted to comfort her during this process, but she'd simply pulled herself up and worked it out. Of course, she'd tried to defend herself all alone initially which had been a huge mistake. There were too many intricacies within the law that she wouldn't know about. He shook his head, shuddering mentally at what would be happening to her right now if Autumn hadn't seen Mia's name on the docket list.

Mia thought she could do it all and in most cases, she was right. But he was damn well going to take on some of that burden. The woman needed to know her limits. Yoga and ice cream weren't going to solve her problems this time.

And then there was last night, he thought, castigating himself one more time. He'd broken one of his sacred rules. Never get involved with a client. Personal feelings and opinions had no place in his line of business. He was hired to keep people out of jail and he was extremely good at it. If he allowed emotions to muck up the process, it was always dangerous.

Once in his car, he dialed Mark who had gone over to Jeff's school to interview the victim's co-workers and subordinates. "What have you got?" Ash asked as he backed up and started driving back to the office.

"Interesting stuff," Mark replied, sounding confused and more than a little frustrated.

Ash knew the feeling. "All I've got over here are about thirty women who are ready to bake cakes with a steel saw inside and three or four men who are ready to marry Mia. Or at least worship at her feet." He didn't laugh at that though. It really pissed him off that those men were so devoted to Mia. Two of them were even married and the other was old enough to be her grandfather! Each one might argue that they were just concerned co-workers, but Ash knew the signs since he was suffering the same fate.

Mark's next comment broke through Ash's irritation with Mia's male co-workers. "I've discovered some interesting comments and opinions here. Meet me at the front of the school and I'll walk you to where I am. You can listen in on what I'm hearing and form your own opinion. I think there's more to the issue here, although I'm just not sure what it is."

This didn't sound good. "I'll be there in fifteen minutes," Ash replied and swung his steering wheel around so he could change directions.

He was at the school ten minutes later, not nearly as impressed with this school as he was with Mia's workplace. Even the outside wasn't as neat and tidy, but perhaps that was because this was a high school where the kids were a bit more rambunctious and harder to discipline than the elementary school kids.

The bell rang indicating that the students should change classes but many simply lingered in the hallways, not appearing to be in any hurry to move on to their next class. Administrators walked down the halls, ordering people to class, but as Ash watched, the kids only waited until the administrator was past them before they leaned right back against their lockers and continued their conversations.

Even one staff member was standing outside the doors to the building smoking a cigarette. Ash had no way of telling if the staff member was a teacher or administrator, but either way, he knew that smoking in and around school buildings was not permitted.

He saw Mark coming down the hallway towards him and headed in that direction. "What's up?" he asked when he was close enough.

Mark looked down at his notes. "Apparently, Mia borrowed several pieces of equipment from the physical education department for an event at her school and they haven't been returned. She also got Jeff to order some audio/visual equipment that was shipped directly to her."

None of that made any sense. Especially since he'd been in her house and her school and there wasn't any audio visual equipment anywhere to be seen. "Why would she order A/V equipment?"

Mark shrugged his shoulders in response. "That's the big question everyone here is asking. They want their stuff back."

His eyes narrowed on Mark's comments. "What do you mean, everyone?" he asked.

Mark scratched his head. "According to several other people, Jeff ordered equipment for the classrooms and gymnasium but Mia convinced him to send it through her so she could be a second accounting system. No one understands the new process, but apparently it started over a year ago and has been ongoing until Jeff disappeared last week."

Ash raised his eyebrows with this news. Mia hadn't said anything about doing any sort of accounting work for her ex-fiance, nor had she ever mentioned being particularly interested in numbers. "I guarantee that she doesn't have any A/V equipment at her house," Ash confirmed but he was looking down at his own notes so he didn't see Mark's surprised reaction to the news that his boss was familiar enough with the interior of their client's house to know about its contents. "So Jeff was ordering school supplies and pushing everything through Mia. How was she paying for the equipment to the vendors? More specifically, why weren't the supplies being ordered through the school board? I would think those things were done by the county's accounting department. I can't even imagine how Jeff had the ability to order supplies, much less dictate his own accounting procedures. Do you have an estimate on the total cost of all that was ordered this way?" Ash asked.

Mark went through his notes, calculating in his mind. "I would estimate about three hundred thousand, but that's just the stuff I've been able to find so far. I'm pretty sure there are more items purchased through Ms. Paulson for the school that haven't arrived yet."

Ash thought about that for a long moment, considering options. "This doesn't really look good for her," he said on a sigh.

Mark nodded his head. "I don't think the police have discovered this information yet. But when they do, it might actually revoke her bail."

Ash's jaw was tense. "I agree. So we have to figure out this latest twist before the police find out."

Mark crossed his arms over his chest and nodded in agreement. "And before the press. They were pretty brutal about her yesterday."

That caught his attention. "What do you mean?" He hadn't seen anything on the news, but then he hadn't watched the news last night either. Nor had he been into his office to get any information from his assistant.

Mark looked up, surprised. "Didn't you read the papers this morning?"

Ash shook his head. "No. I went directly over to Mia's school and started interviewing her co-workers." He looked around once again, seeing the school administrators in their office joking around about something. Not a very efficient work place, he thought with irritation. "What did the papers say?" he asked, still watching the administrators lounging around, drinking coffee and not appearing to be doing the business of the school in any way.

"The papers were talking about her relationship with Jeff. Apparently someone sent them information that she wanted to get back together with him but he wouldn't even talk to her. She became pretty angry with him and started hanging out in front of his school in an effort to get his attention."

Ash's eyebrows rose with that news. "What was the source?" he demanded, thinking of Mia and how soft she'd been earlier this morning. He completely discarded the idea that Mia was stalking her ex-fiancé. He'd heard too many stories about how Jeff was driving Mia crazy with his crazy antics for him to put any credibility towards the newspaper story. That was just another piece to the puzzle.

"The reporter claimed a confidential source so we don't have a name. But the story was pretty derogatory towards someone who teaches kindergarteners."

"Find out the name of that source," he practically snarled. He didn't like anyone maligning Mia's name any further and his mind was already heading towards filing a lawsuit against the reporter for unsubstantiated claims. He then headed into the office and spoke to the high school office staff, charming the ladies as best he could. Within thirty minutes, he had Mark's notes copied and was sitting with several other staff members in the teachers' lounge, talking to teachers on their breaks as well as the administrators who were just taking yet another break from their office responsibilities. "So what can you tell me about Jeff?" he asked, smiling despite his repugnance for their work ethic. He knew that teachers weren't paid nearly what they were worth, but the lack of energy in this group, the sense that none of them really cared about their jobs, made him angry on behalf of the students and parents who were entrusting their children to their care. It was yet another clue into the character of the victim. Jeff didn't appear to be a very motivating leader unlike Mia who inspired almost embarrassing levels of devotion from her supervisors and co-workers.

There was a long silence as each of the occupants looked at one another. No one wanted to speak up and say anything.

"Anyone know Mia Paulson personally?" he asked, taking a different approach.

People seemed more open to discussing his client. "I thought she was very sweet," one man said. "I didn't know she was such a good accountant until Jeff said all purchases should go through her. But I fixed it when I was ordering a new copier for the teacher's work room and made sure the order went through her. Jeff was pretty angry about that mix-up. I hope she's not angry with me as well," he said, leaning forward.

The man seemed almost fearful of his supervisor. And he didn't appear to be holding any ill will towards Mia. Ash continued to discuss the various items that had been purchased, supposedly through Mia so she could ensure that things were accounted for properly. But as the items that had been ordered through her, or sent to her house, or even the school property she'd borrowed from this school for whatever function and hadn't been returned, added up to a very large amount. Mark had found about three hundred thousand dollars but with all the additional items Ash was hearing about now, he suspected that the amount was closer to seven figures.

At the end of two hours and speaking with several other teachers who rotated through the teachers' lounge, he thought he had a good idea of what was happening.

He just had to prove it now. Embezzlement was always a tough crime to prove, but he'd won harder cases than this.

"Mia, I need you over at my office," he said as soon as she picked up the phone. "We have a problem and need your help."

As soon as he walked into his office, he called a meeting to reveal the latest. He caught Mia's eye and wished she didn't look so nervous. But he couldn't stop to reassure her now. There was too much to do and he was racing against the clock as it was. As soon as the teachers realized that the press and the police didn't have this information, they would notify them. And he'd bet the police were going to show up here to arrest Mia. He had to get her out of this mess before that happened. And that meant he needed to get things figured out.

What a mess, he thought.

Mia looked across the busy office at Ash, wishing he would slow down and tell her what was going on. He had left her house early this morning before she'd woken. After the previous night, she'd wanted to wake up in his arms and feel that wonderful heat. But looking at him now, he looked so grim! Had she made a mistake? Why hadn't she gone with her intelligence last night instead of just letting her body rule her decisions? Over and over again, she'd told herself that Ash didn't believe in her. He thought she was a murderer but the last few days and especially last night, he'd been different. He'd been kind and gentle.

She thought about that night he'd followed her when she'd snuck out to get ice cream. He'd probably thought she was going to rob the convenience store! She'd disproved him that night and all the evidence the prosecuting attorney had against her was circumstantial. Ash had told her last night that he thought the charges would be dropped, so what was wrong now?

Why was he looking so angry?

She curled her arms around her, feeling scared and cold. He barely even looked at her. It was almost as if he couldn't bear to look at her, embarrassed that he'd slept with her last night.

Damn him! Why wouldn't he talk to her? He'd interrogated her over and over again during the past several days, why was he not talking to her now? If he'd discovered something new, something horrible, she should be the first one to hear it, shouldn't she?

She watched him walk across the room, talk something over with Mark and nod his head. He was so painfully handsome and strong. She sighed to herself, wishing she hadn't made such a fool of herself over him last night. She should have been more reserved. She should have stayed away from him.

So what if he'd been a sweetheart about her yard? She suspected he'd been the one to order all those pizzas for everyone. It suddenly occurred to her that a large truck had been pulling away from the curb when she'd come around from the backyard. That must have been where the mulch had come from! Had Ash ordered that as well?

If he had, she'd pay him back for every penny! She wasn't going to be beholden to a man who didn't believe in her innocence. This was ridiculous! The man was her lawyer. She should just maintain professional distance from him.

But even as she told herself that, her eyes hungrily watched him. He handed papers to one of the other lawyers, both of them discussing whatever information was on that paper.

She pulled her wallet out of her purse and wrote a check. When she was finished, she stormed over to him, her body shaking with her hurt and anger. "Here!" she snapped to him, holding out the check.

Ash looked down at her, seeing the vulnerability in her eyes. As much as he wanted to pull her into his arms and reassure her, he couldn't slow down. Jean had gotten a message from the district attorney, but he hadn't called back. It could only be bad news at this point. Good news would be the charges being dropped and that would most likely come in a formal notice as well as a call. Since it was only a phone call, he was fighting against the clock.

"What's this?" he asked, trying to focus on her, but he stopped to shout an order over to one of the investigators, "Get me a list of all the equipment." And then something else occurred to him so he put a hand on her shoulder, wincing when she stepped out of his reach. "Mark, look into storage units. And do another check on bank accounts. You know what we're looking for. We need to find it before the police to have better control over the information."

When Mark hurried off to his computers, his efficient fingers already flying over the keyboard, Ash turned back to Mia, looking down at her once again. "Sorry. What's this about?" he asked, waving the check in his hand.

"That's for the pizza and mulch yesterday. If that doesn't cover the expenses, please ask Jean to give me a revised amount. I'll pay it."

Someone handed him something else and he looked at it quickly. "This is good. Hand this to Mark. He's looking into stuff like this."

He sighed and looked back down at her. "Mia, why would you think I wanted a check for anything? And why do you think I paid for the pizza?"

"And the mulch," she said belligerently and moved even farther away from him. She couldn't be too close. She might just throw herself into his arms and beg him to save her. She didn't want to be saved. She could do this on her own.

"Mia, I'm not letting you pay for anything. Would you just hold on?" he asked, taking her arms before she could move even farther away from him. She kept inching away as if he were contaminated somehow. And after last night, it irritated him beyond words.

"You can't just…" she sniffed and shook her head. "Just stop. I'm not letting you do this," she said firmly and started to turn away. She had to get out of there. She would hire another lawyer. There had to be others in the Chicago area that were as good, or even better, than Ash Thorpe.

"You're not letting me do what?" he demanded, turning his full attention to her, hands on his hips as he glared down at her.

Mia refused to be intimidated by his angry attitude. He might be taller and stronger, but she wasn't bowing down to his glare. "All of this," she waved, indicating the numerous people around her who were rushing about, trying to solve this puzzle. "I want it to stop. I'll find someone else. Someone who believes in me and doesn't think I'm a criminal."

Ash stared at her, stunned. He wasn't sure what to say to get it through to her, but more importantly, he could almost feel the police and district attorney as they bore down on the details he'd discovered earlier today. "Mia…" he started to say, but shook his head. Instead, he grabbed her arm and pulled her into his office. Slamming the door, he pulled her into his arms, kissing her. She resisted for only a moment before he felt her arms go around his neck and his body relaxed somewhat.

The relaxation lasted only a moment before her soft body and the delicious taste of her hit him full force. He'd meant to just give her the most expedient reassurance he could, but that plan had backfired on him as soon as he'd taken her into his arms. As was always the case when he touched her, the intense heat of his desire inflamed his senses and it took every ounce of willpower to pull back. "You're not going anywhere," he told her firmly.

He took her hand and pulled her out of his office, smiling with the stunned and flustered look in her eyes which told him he hadn't been the only one who had been thrown by that kiss.

"Okay everyone! We need to get things in order. Bring whatever you have to the conference room," he called out.

When everyone was assembled, he looked around. "Mark, tell everyone what you discovered."

Mark swiveled in the leather chair so he was looking at more of the group. "We found that there was approximately one point two million dollars in school equipment and hardware that was ordered ostensibly through Ms. Paulson. That's not counting the equipment that everyone assumed Ms. Paulson had borrowed but hasn't yet been returned."

That captured Mia's attention and she leaned forward, obviously ready to argue her side of things but Ash held up his hand, silently asking her to hold off for the moment. Mia snapped her mouth closed, irritated that he wasn't even letting her defend herself! How rude! And arrogant, she thought, leaning back against the irritatingly comfortable leather chair and glaring at the man.

Ash ignored her irritation and continued to look at Mark. "Do you have a breakdown of what was borrowed versus which items were bought and never delivered?" he asked.

Mia shook her head. "I never…"

Ash stopped her yet again and Mia sat back in her chair with a huff. She glared at Ash, furious that he wouldn't let her talk.

After all they'd shared last night, she had thought that he was starting to care for her. She was so furious with herself for falling for his charm. Damn him! She'd believed in him! She'd believed they could share something together.

Okay, so they'd known each other for only a few days. And all of those days, he'd been defending her on murder charges. Add to that, she was a thief now.

Good grief, she didn't even know how to order some of these supplies, much less what they were. She was a kindergarten school teacher! What did she need with football equipment she thought mutinously as Mark read through the list of the items he'd discovered which had been borrowed? And why on earth would she tell Jeff that she needed that equipment for a field day at her school? They had their own equipment! High school sports equipment was too big for elementary aged children. Even the basketballs were smaller!

She crossed her arms over her chest, tapping her foot with impatience at how ludicrous this story was. Not to mention how betrayed she felt when she realized that Ash wasn't even arguing that she hadn't borrowed or stolen any of this equipment. He was being very clinical about the entire discussion while she sat here fuming with fury.

After last night, she would have thought that he trusted her more. But the way he was treating her, he was acting like she was a worse criminal than before. As if being a murderer versus a murderer as well as a thief….she stopped and thought about that. Okay, being a murderer versus a thief was worse. Taking a life was much more reprehensible than stealing material things. Not that she would do either, but still…she had to admit that murder ranked higher up on the "badness" scale than embezzlement and theft.

She crossed her legs, the top one swinging back and forth with impatience and anger. Her mind was whirling, trying to figure out why someone would even say that about her. She didn't really know the teachers and administrators over at Jeff's school. Of course, she'd met them at social functions. Jeff was the principal so as his girlfriend and fiancée, she'd had a few opportunities where she'd interacted with his staff.

She gasped. "That gives me motive!" she exclaimed, sitting up straight, her worried eyes moving to Ash's, begging him for reassurance.

Ash shook his head one more time and turned back to his team. "Kiera? It looks like you might have something."

The new lawyer on the team nodded her head, her eyes skimming over the report she'd pulled right before the meeting. Kiera's eyes were in a quandary. "I might. I started looking into Ms. Knightley's financials, like you asked," she explained.

That couldn't be good news, she thought, a lump forming in her throat and her stomach starting to twist into knots. "I didn't do this, Ash," she whispered up to him, begging him to believe her.

His only response was to place a firm hand on her shoulder, silently telling her to keep quiet.

She jerked her arm free and shook her head. "No! I won't shut up!" she cried out, furious with him and also with herself for putting herself into this kind of a position. She'd thought Jeff was nice and sweet. As soon as she'd figured him out, she'd tried hard to get out of his clutches but she'd been too naïve to do the right thing. Now the same thing was happening with Ash and she felt duped once again. She wasn't going to put up with it any longer.

She stood up and glared at Ash, desperately fighting for him to believe in her. To believe she wouldn't do these kinds of things. "I tried to get away from him," she explained to Ash, fighting back the tears and the panic. "And after..." she stopped herself, her body straining not to punch his arm because she did not believe in violence but there was a limit to a person's control. And right now, he was straining at her limits.

She couldn't say anything else without breaking down and she definitely didn't want to do that in front of all these people. "I have to get out of here," she said, realizing that everyone was staring at her, waiting for her to finish that sentence.

Before she embarrassed herself and broke down in tears, she rushed out of the conference room.

"Mia!" Ash called out, wanting to go after her, but his gut was telling him that whatever Kiera had to say was important.

He sighed, running a hand through his hair in frustration. He'd catch up with her once he'd figured this out. Everything inside of him was telling him to ignore the evidence against Mia. It just didn't jive with what he knew of her character. He was fully aware that people weren't always what they appeared to be, but he simply couldn't believe that she could so completely fool him.

Besides, she had an enormous army of people who were supporting her. Worst case scenario, he pulled in every single one of her co-workers and neighbors as character witnesses. Each one of them could give a story about what Mia had done to help them. Hell, she didn't have time to do any of the crap people were now saying about her because she was always baking a cake for someone, making soup for a sick person or helping someone in some other way.

No, Mia didn't embezzle over a million dollars from the school system. And she definitely didn't murder her ex-fiancé. He would bet his career on it. Hell, he was betting his life on it.

He smiled at the thought. Yes, he was going to have a pretty long, happy life. Filled with surprises and saved earthworms, but he could handle that. He wouldn't push the spiders out of the house though. Those things were road kill and she'd just have to get over it.

He looked back at the group with grim determination. "Okay, Kiera, whatcha got?" he prompted.

Kiera shifted in her chair. "This is just preliminary, mind you. I was looking through the data yesterday and found nothing, but something caught my attention this morning. Mia's finances are spotless. There's no evidence of any additional bank accounts, her expenses are miniscule except for the purchase of her house. All of her expenditures match the income of a school teacher with her level of experience. So I looked further into Jeff's finances. When I didn't find anything, I went on to his relatives and anyone who was close to him." She looked down at her papers and pulled one out. "Jeff's new fiancée is a nurse," she said carefully, passing the paper over to Ash. "Nurses make a good salary," she cautioned, "but I'm not sure they can afford a brand new, black BMW with all the bells and whistles."

Ash looked up sharply from the paper. "BMW?"

Kiera nodded confidently. "Bought the day after Ms. Paulson was arrested," she added.

Ash's face looked serious as he read through the details of the woman's purchase. But when his eyes fixed on the price, his eyes cleared. When he saw the date, he stood up and his face cleared of worry.

"Ladies and gentleman, I think we just found a new suspect in the murder of Jeff Richardson," he said.

Leslie, one of Mark's investigators rushed into the conference room, out of breath and obviously a bit frazzled. "Sir?"

Ash turned away from the conference room windows, trying to push his worry away from Mia. Focusing back on the group, he looked at Leslie, nodding his head for her to go ahead. "What did you find?"

Leslie pushed some pictures towards the center of the table. "You asked me to sit on the new fiancée," she said. With a grin, she pulled the most important one out of the pile.

Ash picked up the pictures she'd taken of the woman's house and looked at them, his smile growing when he realized what he was seeing. "And this is what you saw?" he asked, but it wasn't really a question since he was staring at the evidence.

Leslie nodded her head with a huge grin on her face. "I couldn't get a good shot," she cautioned, "but I'm pretty sure that's Jeff Richardson."

Ash was just about to laugh when a commotion outside the conference room caught his attention. Just as he'd anticipated, there were four police officers standing in the reception area.

Ash took the two pictures and walked out of the conference room.

Mia watched with growing terror as the police officers spotted her and moved in her direction. There were four of them! Did they really think she was going to run?

She held onto the desk behind her, her whole body feeling faint. This couldn't be happening! It was simply a nightmare and she was trapped in sleep, desperately fighting to wake up.

As the police officers came closer, she knew that it wasn't a dream. This was a nightmare, of course, but it was a real life nightmare in which she was about to be arrested, her bond revoked because everyone thought she had stolen over one million dollars from the school system and had the means to flee the country.

She didn't even have a passport!

And then Ash was there, his strong body placed between her and the police officers.

"Gentleman, you can't arrest Ms. Paulson for a murder that she didn't commit," Ash was saying.

"Mr. Thorpe," one of them, obviously the one in charge, had his hand on his gun. "I appreciate your efforts on behalf of your client, but we have a warrant for her arrest on suspicion of embezzlement. A judge signed the order just after lunchtime and her bail has been revoked."

Ash was shaking his head and holding up a picture. "You can't arrest someone for a crime that hasn't even been committed yet," he was saying.

Mia was completely confused. She tried to peer around Ash's shoulders, but his hand pushed her right back behind him. She should be irritated, but he was being protective and she kind of liked that. It might be old-fashioned, but in this one situation, she preferred being protected by a huge, heavy handed, supremely intelligent man who obviously had some sort of get-out-of-jail-free card. Because the police officers were staring at the photograph carefully.

"Is that...?" one of them started to ask.

"Yes, gentlemen, that is Jeff Richardson in the kitchen of his current fiancée." He pulled up another picture, one of a sleek, shiny new car. "And this is Ms. Knightley's new car, purchased, in cash, one day after Ms. Paulson was arrested."

Leslie came closer and handed him another photograph. "I know the first picture is a bit blurry, so here's a clearer picture of the two of them from their engagement photograph."

The police officers looked at the first, then the third picture, obviously confused.

"Where did you get that photograph?" a new voice chimed in.

Everyone turned to face a blond woman approaching the officers fearlessly. She snatched the photo out of the officer's hands and turned around. "Are you having me followed?" she demanded of Ryker Thorpe who was walking up behind her, a look of mild irritation on his handsome features.

"Why would you ask that?" he demanded. "Do you know the man in that photograph?"

Cricket glared up at the man, her irritation increasing as she lifted the photo up higher. "These two people are the heads of the charity my boss wants me to look into as a tax deduction. I was with them yesterday afternoon. Are you telling me you haven't had someone following me?"

Ash stepped in front of the blond beauty but his brother pushed him out of the way. Ash didn't have time to castigate his oldest brother right at the moment. He had to clarify this latest twist. "I don't know who you are…" he started to say.

Ryker interrupted him. "This is Cricket Fairchild. She's one of my clients."

The woman rolled her eyes. "Okay, so now that we've established who I am, would someone mind telling me why you are investigating the person I'm investigating?"

The police officer stepped in at that moment. "Ma'am, are you telling me that you were with this man yesterday afternoon?"

Cricket nodded her head, causing her blond curls to dance merrily around her stunning features. "I was with both of them. Isn't that what I just said? It was a lunch meeting at their request," she explained. "He ordered steak and she had some sort of disgusting fish meal."

"And you would be willing to testify to this?" the officer asked.

Cricket looked around, her green eyes trying to figure out why everyone was tense. "Of course. Why? Has someone bankrupted his charity or something? They're very passionate about saving the whales off the coast of Greenland."

Ash watched with amusement as his older brother rolled his eyes. "Cricket, the police believe this man was murdered last week."

She laughed and shook her head. "No. He wasn't murdered last week. He was giving me a pitch to help him fund the next ship they are trying to acquire."

Ryker looked over her head at his younger brother. "I think that sort of clinches things for you doesn't it?" he asked, a smile in his eyes as he glanced back to the brunette.

Ash was grinning broadly. "Pretty much," he said and turned to the officers. "Do you need anything else?" he asked them.

The officers shook their heads in amazement but they were all grinning. "We're all good here, Mr. Thorpe."

"Call me Ash," he said, slapping one of them on the arm jovially. "I think there are cupcakes in the break room," he offered. "Stop by and grab one. I've heard they're fantastic."

Mia bit her lip, her whole body waiting tensely. She only started to relax when one of the officers nodded politely to her. "I think we'd better skip the cupcake for now but we'll take a rain check. Can I have these two pictures?" he asked.

Ash quickly nodded. "Let me know if you need additional copies. We're more than happy to print more for you."

The police officer took the pictures, but hesitated in front of the blond woman. Ryker immediately understood what they were afraid to ask and stepped in to reassure all four of them. "Ms. Fairchild will make a statement if you need one," Ryker was offering.

"I will?" Cricket asked, looking up at the man she seemed to dislike intensely. "What will I be stating?"

"That you had lunch with a murder victim yesterday," he stated succinctly, not clearing up any of the woman's confusion before he took her arm and led her back down the hallway. "Come along. You and I have a lot to discuss."

Mia watched with fascination as the oldest of the Thorpe brothers dragged the beautiful woman down the hallway. She obviously didn't want to go, but she didn't fight him either.

Mia's smile started off small. But as the realization hit her, that grin expanded over her entire face, growing in intensity and she was almost light-headed with the relief that surged through her. And she was startled when the blond woman smiled brightly right back at her, waving her fingers in the air before she disappeared around the corner.

"In my office," Ash snapped at her.

Mia jumped and tore her eyes away from the disappearing blond woman and looked up at Ash. Gone was that feeling of freedom that had been starting to bubble up inside of her. All that anger she'd felt only moments ago surged right back to the front of her mind. "I'm not..." she started to say but Ash didn't wait for her to respond. He moved in closer, his face barely an inch from hers.

"Don't say another word, Mia. Just go right into my office. We have some things to discuss and I'm definitely not going to do them in front of my staff."

Mia pulled back slightly and looked around. Sure enough, just about every person in the area was frozen in place, waiting to see what she would do. No one disobeyed a direct command from Ash Thorpe. But some of them suspected that she might. She could see the hope in their eyes.

Unfortunately, she didn't have the courage to ignore him either. At least not this time.

She stepped back and marched into his office, just about to slam the door behind her when she felt it stop.

Swinging around, she glared at him, her hands on her hips defiantly while she watched him walk into his office behind her.

She waited a fraction of a second for his office door to slam closed before she started in on him. "Don't you dare ever speak to me like that!" she almost yelled. "I can't believe I slept with you last night!" she said, this time her voice definitely was louder. "I can't believe I let you into my house, that I thought I was in love with you and I slept with you!" Her hands went into her hair. "Good grief, there was almost no sleeping anyway! So I can't really say that, can I? No, I had to go sleep with the enemy! Not that you're really the enemy," she clarified for herself, pacing back and forth in his office, her fury rising higher as she contemplated all that she'd messed up in her life. "I was such a wimp! I can't believe it, every time you touched me, I thought you were feeling the same thing I felt! I thought that you cared for me! When all that time, you were just having a good old time, weren't you? And all that time, you thought I was not just a murderer, but a thief! And a thief who steals from the schools! The kids! I'm a horrible human being because I steal money that the kids need for their education. It isn't bad enough that some of them can't even afford clothes or food, but now there's a horrible woman who is stealing the equipment right out from under them."

She was really working herself up into a good lather now. "And I wasn't even smart about it! No! A smart thief would have used an alias to embezzle the funds. I had to use my own name." She gasped and turned around. "I can't believe you thought I was so stupid that I wouldn't know how to embezzle money!" She realized how ridiculous that sounded and shook her head. "Okay, so maybe I don't know how to embezzle money, but believe me, I'm not so stupid as to use my own name!"

"I know," Ash said softly, leaning against his door with his arms crossed over his chest, just watching her work herself up in anger.

She didn't listen to him, going on and on about how she'd been such a sap last night. "And believe it or not, I was actually hurt this morning when I woke up and found you no longer in bed." She slapped her forehead with exasperation at her naiveté. "I actually made excuses for you! I had this all worked out in my mind that you just figured something out in the middle of the night and left early, letting me sleep in because I was exhausted from the nightmare of the last few days. But all you were doing was finding more evidence of my crimes!"

The door opened and both of them turned to look at Ash's administrative assistant poke her head in. "I'm sorry to interrupt," she said, her face red for some reason, "but the DA is on the phone and wants to talk to you. He said it is urgent and he didn't sound happy."

Ash turned to look at Mia. "Stay here. We have more to discuss," he said and walked out the door, giving her privacy in the hopes that she would calm down.

As soon as he left, the middle aged woman stepped inside, carrying a cup of coffee. "I thought you might need this," she said softly. "I'm Jeanie," she said. "I think we'll be getting to know each other very well soon."

Mia took the cup gratefully and took a fortifying sip. "Thank you," she whispered, all of her energy gone now that her target was no longer in sight. "I appreciate the coffee, but I really need to get out of here."

Jeanie was quiet for a long moment, looking at the gorgeous brunette with understanding. "You're wrong about him," she said in a soothing tone of voice.

Mia halted her pacing and stopped to turn to the kind woman. "I'm sorry?" she asked.

Jeannie smiled gently. "You're wrong. About Mr. Thorpe."

Mia shook her head. "How do you…"

The kind woman smiled gently and took a step closer, as if she needed to emphasize her next words. "Mr. Thorpe never gets involved in investigations," she explained. "He manages at a high level, working on trial strategy, overseeing more than twenty different cases. He goes to court representing clients in only a small number of those cases." She let those words sink in before continuing. "Mr. Thorpe was at the school this morning interviewing your co-workers. He then went over to the high school after Mark called him about some odd issues."

That irritated her. "I know. That's where he started to think I was a thief as well."

Jeannie smiled and looked down, trying to figure out how to help this beautiful, young woman understand her point. "This case was different," she tried a different approach. "It wasn't that Mr. Thorpe was trying to get you acquitted."

Mia took a deep breath and tried to listen, tried to understand her point. "He always tries to get people acquitted. That's his job."

"Exactly. Mr. Thorpe wasn't trying to get you acquitted. He was trying to prove your innocence."

Mia knew the kind woman was trying to tell her something important but she just wasn't getting it. "I'm sorry, I'm just not getting your point."

Jeannie laughed. "Mr. Thorpe is a high level director. People hire him from all over the country because he's the best at getting people acquitted."

"That just means he doesn't care where he gets his money as long as he's still raking it in."

Jeannie once again shook her head. "You misunderstand. The man you're in love with has one of the highest codes of honor I've ever experienced in this business. Mr. Thorpe doesn't take cases when he's sure the defendant is guilty."

With those words, Jeannie turned and walked out of the office, leaving Mia to think about what had been revealed.

She was exhausted from a night of not sleeping well, plus the stress of the past several days. She wasn't sure what was going on and didn't completely understand what Ash's assistant had been trying to say.

Unfortunately, or maybe it was a good thing, because Autumn rushed into the office and grabbed Mia into a bear hug. "I just heard the news!" she screamed. "I'm so relieved. I told you Ash could get you out of this mess!" she said, rocking back and forth with her arms around Mia's shoulders.

Mia laughed and tried to nod her head, but Autumn's grip was too tight. "You were right. He got everything all cleared up. I can't believe it's actually over!"

Autumn laughed, delighted. "We have to go out and celebrate!" she exclaimed. "Let's go do Durango's!"

"Yes!" Mia agreed, knowing that a margarita was exactly what she needed right now. She needed to work her mind through Jeanie's comments, not completely understanding what she'd been trying to say. Perhaps she was too emotionally charged at this point. She needed to relax and wrap her mind around the fact that prison wasn't looming in her future. "I'm totally in!" She didn't tell her friend that she wanted to just drink herself free of the confusing man. Nor did she tell Autumn that her boss had told Mia to stay in his office. She wasn't going to listen to him, still feeling betrayed after last night.

It occurred to her that she should be more grateful to Ash. Without his help, she would be in a jail cell right now. His investigators had discovered the truth and he'd had the skills to put it all together. But staying here where he would come back and confuse her even more was not a good idea. She never thought clearly when Ash was around so it was better to figure things out far away from him.

She stopped when she was out in the open and looked around at all the smiling faces. "Thank you everyone," she said softly, but with sincerity. "Thank you so much for figuring this out. I'm so grateful to all of you for your efforts. All of you are amazing people!" she said. Everyone smiled right back at her, some raising their coffee cups in salute and she bowed her head in respect to their success.

Autumn pulled Mia out of the office, waving to the crowd as well, each of them celebrating for a moment before they moved on to the next case. She stopped at Jeannie's desk. "If Ash is looking for Mia, tell him I've kidnapped her and taken her to Durango's, okay?"

Jeannie's smile widened in approval. "Will do. Have one for me!"

Autumn hesitated and smiled right back. "Want to come along and celebrate?"

Jeannie waved her hand. "Thanks but I'm leaving early today so I can get my kids to a dentist appointment. Go ahead and have a great time. Make sure she relaxes," she told Autumn, referring to Mia who was obviously not as relaxed as she should be in the face of her absolution from the crimes she'd been accused of less than a week ago.

Autumn looked down at Mia, then back at Jeanie before saying, "Definitely."

At the elevator, Autumn and Mia were laughing, the realization that Mia was truly free slowly sinking in.

"Men!" the pretty, blond woman sighed as she pressed the elevator call button over and over. Mia and Autumn watched her touch the diamond ring on her finger reverently, then shake her head. Mia looked at Autumn and both women nodded at the same time, obviously having the exact same idea.

Mia smiled at the woman with genuine appreciation. "You're the woman who just helped me stay out of jail," Mia said. "Are you okay?"

Cricket spun around and noticed the two lovely women behind her. "I'm sorry," she said and took a deep breath while closing her eyes. "Nothing a good martini can't fix," she said, trying to calm down. "Men are just so confusing!" she snapped, the calming breath obviously not working too well.

Mia knew the feeling. "Why don't you come with us? I don't know about the martinis," she cautioned, "but the margaritas at Durango's are perfect for anything that ails you."

Cricket considered the option. She didn't know these two women, but she could definitely use a night on the town with some women her own age. "I'm not sure I should be around humanity right now," she came back.

Mia laughed. "That's exactly where I am. I'm Mia Paulson," she said. "And we're heading out to celebrate me not being in jail for the rest of my life."

Cricket smiled back, taking Mia's hand in hers. "That sounds like a perfect start to the weekend. I think I'll join you after all."

The three women walked out the door and headed down the sidewalk to the bar that was down the street from the office. They found a table in the back of the bar and settled down, ordering a huge pitcher of margaritas with three glasses.

When they were all poured with chips and salsa in the middle of the table, Autumn raised her glass in the air. "To avoiding jail time and men!" she said with emphatic conviction.

Mia was just about to raise her glass when she spotted another woman sitting alone at the bar. "Wait!" she called out, moments before they took a sip. "That woman, her name is Kira or Kiera, right?"

Autumn looked over at the bar and nodded. "Yes. She's the new lawyer on Ash's team. She started the day you were arrested."

Mia's grin grew wider as she watched the sad looking woman sitting off to the side at one of the darker tables. "She's the one who found the information about Jeff's current fiancée buying the new BMW."

Without another word, Autumn stood up and walked over to the woman who looked as sad and miserable as Mia felt at the moment.

Cricket and Mia watched as Autumn spoke softly to the other woman, gesturing in their direction. Mia knew instantly what was going on and she grabbed a chair from the next table, bringing it over to their own.

"Hi Kiera!" she called out, signaling to the waiter to bring another glass. "Looks like you're in the same boat as the rest of us so you might as well join us," she said and poured the woman a drink.

Kiera smiled gratefully and introduced herself to Cricket. "So back to where we were before," Cricket said, lifting her glass one more time. "To no jail time and no obnoxious men!"

The three other women laughed, but they all clinked glasses and took a long sip of the sweet and sour mixture, laughing about the men they'd dated in the past. Mia didn't bring up the fact that she was personally involved with Ash. She thought that would be a bit too revealing, but she thought it was interesting that Cricket reviled Ash's older brother Ryker. And Mia knew that Autumn was refusing to date any of the men she introduced her to but she was quite adamant that Xander Thorpe was the worst of the four Thorpe brothers. Which struck Mia as very interesting.

And it could just be the tequila finally hitting her system, but Mia thought it was fascinating that the lovely brunette lawyer looked down at her drink anytime one of the brothers was mentioned. Was the beautiful Kiera interested in another man? Or perhaps one that had already been mentioned? Mia watched her carefully and knew something was up when the slender woman held her breath at the mere mention of Axel Thorpe. Bingo, Mia thought and sat back, mentally congratulating herself on figuring out what was going on.

Two hours later, they were on their third pitcher of drinks and the four women were tight friends. "So what's up with the boss man?" Cricket asked, laughing as she grabbed another chip.

"You mean Ryker?" Autumn asked, taking a long gulp of her margarita despite the fact that the room was already swaying.

Cricket also took a long, satisfying swallow of her icy drink and nodded. "Or more appropriately referred to as the most obnoxious, irritating, domineering and arrogant man on the planet."

Autumn laughed and shook her head. "He's not so bad," she said. "You haven't met Xander yet if you think Ryker is bad. Xander's a jerk!"

"Oh crap!" Mia gasped, her drink frozen halfway to her lips.

Cricket looked over. "What's wrong?"

Her glass dropped to the table with a clink. "I just realized that I'm in love with the horrible man!"

Kiera smiled, having figured that one out about three drinks ago. "And? Sounds like we all have man troubles."

Mia, Autumn and Cricket all looked at their new best friend. "You too?" they gasped almost in unison.

Autumn's eyes narrowed. She looked around at counted. When she came to the right conclusion, she too gasped in horror. "No!"

Mia was having trouble keeping up. "What?" Were they talking about the Thorpe brothers still? She was a little fuzzy now.

Cricket laughed and shook her head. "Figures," she said and poured Kiera another glass.

"What?" Mia asked again, but took a sip while she looked over the rim of her glass.

Autumn threw back her head and laughed. "I can't believe it! You too?"

Kiera sighed and took a long sip of her drink as well.

Mia cringed she voiced the conclusion she'd come to a couple of hours ago. "Axel?" she asked, instantly feeling sorry for the poor woman.

Kiera's shoulders shrugged slightly. "Everyone has their albatross."

The four men standing behind the table listened with only slightly veiled amusement. Axel rolled his eyes when he was referred to as an albatross. "At least I wasn't referred to as obnoxious, irritating and domineering."

"Don't forget arrogant," Xander piped up, filling in the one adjective his brother had forgotten.

Ryker rolled his eyes. "You're the one that was most recently referred to as a jerk, if you recall."

Xander pushed away from the bar and put his half-drunk beer down on the bar behind him. "I think it's time to crash this party. Don't you gentlemen?"

Ryker completely agreed. "I'll get their tab. Who is going to be the first to break things up before we're tarred and feathered?"

He turned around and gestured to the ladies' waiter, handing him a credit card to cover their drinks for the night.

Ash was the first to step in, starting to move in behind Mia but Autumn's next words stopped him several feet from their table. He didn't move, just waited for more interesting information to be revealed.

"What were you saying 'crap' earlier? You and Ash are great together," Autumn commented, leaning back, completely oblivious to the four extremely large men warily approaching their table.

Mia shrugged and took another long sip of her drink. "Oh, nothing important. I just really don't want to be in love with my jerk."

The three women stopped drinking and stared hard. "Are you kidding?" Autumn asked, a huge grin on her face.

Mia's eyes narrowed as something occurred to her. She stared hard at her friend, her mind trying to work despite all the alcohol that was making everything fuzzy. "Did you have this planned already?" she asked.

Autumn laughed, delighted. "Not at all. When I saw your name on the docket, I didn't spare a moment to consider anything, but remember that last time you came by to pick me up for yoga?" she asked.

Mia nodded her head, already suspicious. "What about it?"

"You were late. You were supposed to come up and get me. And I was going to have you accidentally run into Ash."

Mia gasped. "You sneaky…! Why would you do that to me?"

Autumn smiled. "What's the problem? You're already in love with him."

"Yeah, but he's not in love with me. And besides, he doesn't trust me."

"Yes he does," Autumn contradicted.

"Yes, I do," A deep voice interrupted.

Mia spun around and groaned.

"What are you doing here?" she demanded, almost spilling her drink as her hand started shaking. "Go away. You don't trust me and I'm not going to be in love with a man who doesn't trust me."

Ash didn't even bother to reply to that. He simply took the glass out of her hand and bent down to lift her into his arms. Walking out of the restaurant, he nodded to his brothers who were starting to move in on what he suspected were their women. Or at least what he hoped were the women these men had been grouching over. He was at least relieved to see that Xander was moving in on Autumn's chair but didn't take the time to wonder what would happen between the two of them. He had too much to worry about with this one.

"Put me down," she grumbled. "I'm too heavy for you to carry me," she said and laid her head down on his broad shoulder.

Ash raised an eyebrow at that, but didn't slow down at all. He wanted her in his brownstone where he could strip off this ugly suit she'd chosen to wear and find all that lovely softness he knew was underneath. He was going to spend the rest of the evening and all of the night convincing her that he trusted her, had always trusted her and would always trust her in the future and she needed to marry him as soon as possible.

"I'm hiring a new lawyer," she said while he was tucking her into the passenger seat of his car.

"Of course you are," he said and strapped her seat belt on.

Her eyes narrowed on his amused face but she suspected the action might be diminished since she was having trouble focusing on him. "You might be big and gorgeous," she said with a sigh as she laughed when he tickled her, "but I can resist you easily."

"Think so?" he replied, not believing a word of it. Nice to hear that she thought he was gorgeous, he thought.

"Absolutely! You don't trust me. That's easy to resist."

"I trust you," he countered, but slammed the door so she couldn't argue with him any longer.

He chuckled as he walked around to the driver's seat. So the woman thought he was 'gorgeous'? He liked that.

Sliding into the car, he started it up and backed out of the parking space, glancing in her direction to see if she was okay. Her eyes were closed and she had a satisfied look on her lovely features, just like she had last night when he'd been making love to her.

"And you're not getting another lawyer," he said softly, thinking she'd fallen asleep after all the margaritas she'd imbibed.

He was wrong. Her widening smile indicated as much. "You can't stop me," she came right back, not bothering to open her eyes.

He chuckled as he drove through the streets of downtown Chicago. "Why would you need a new lawyer? Are you planning to let some earthworms die off on the sidewalk?"

That wiped her smile away and she turned to glare at him. "I'll have you know that earthworms are a very important part of our ecosystem. And because of that, they're one of the very best composters. You want gorgeous plants and flowers, get a bunch of worms."

He laughed and shook his head. "Are we talking about our relationship or worm dung?" he asked, confidently maneuvering through the streets.

"We don't have a relationship. So let's talk about worm…" she hesitated to use the other term so she just said, "poop."

"We definitely have a relationship. And I'll make sure you don't get a new lawyer."

She laughed as if his statement as well as his confidence were outrageous. "How do you think you're going to stop me?" she asked, snuggling down into the soft leather seat. "And stop being charming. I don't like you." Worry lines appeared on her forehead and she turned to look up at him. "I can't remember why at the moment, but it will come to me."

"You think I don't trust you," he told her with a wink.

"Right!" she said, trying to snap her fingers but they wouldn't connect properly for some reason. After several failed attempts, she simply waved her hands and then let them fall onto her lap.

"Autumn is in love with Xander, isn't she?" Mia asked, squinting through the darkened windshield.

"That's our theory. But no one will touch it and question either party to find out why they won't do anything about it."

Mia mulled that over in her mind. "I don't think I have the courage either."

Ash laughed, shaking his head. "Mia, you're one of the bravest women I know."

She blinked, not sure she'd heard him correctly. "That was possibly the sweetest thing anyone has ever said to me."

He braked for a red light and looked down at her. "We're getting married, you know."

Mia rolled her eyes. "And there goes the sweetness and charm." She shrugged philosophically. "I figured as much. Only an ogre would ask a woman to marry her in such an outrageous manner."

He chuckled again. "You've already told me I'm gorgeous and charming."

"I never said charming," she came right back. "And I didn't say gorgeous."

"I heard gorgeous," he countered.

"I never will admit to saying gorgeous." With that she sighed and leaned back in the leather seat one more time. "And where are you taking me?" she demanded, trying to figure out where they were. "I'm not going back to your brownstone," she told him firmly. "I need to go home."

"You're going to have to sell your pretty house, Mia. I can't live in a house with a blue kitchen. We've already discussed that."

"I'm not selling my house, I'm not living with you and so your masculinity is safe from my kitchen, which is periwinkle. Not blue."

He couldn't believe she was arguing about the color of her kitchen when he'd just proposed to her. Albeit in a rather unromantic manner. Even he had to admit that telling someone they were going to get married was rather unromantic. But hell, she was talking about getting a new lawyer! What was a man supposed to do?

Not that he was threatened at all. The woman was too wholesome for words. He couldn't imagine another bizarre situation where she would need a lawyer. So the point was mute anyway. "You're coming to my house, and I'll try to be more romantic once the alcohol has worn off. How's that?"

She immediately shook her head. "I'm not going back to your house," she stated firmly once again. "I'm going to my house and I'm going to have breakfast in my periwinkle kitchen and I'll sleep in my flowered sheets and you can't do anything to stop me."

Since they were already parked in his garage, he'd like to know how she was going to get home. But he didn't point that out to her. He simply got out of the car and walked around to her side, intending to lift her out of the seat again and carry her into his house where she belonged.

Instead, she was standing, rather unsteadily, beside his car and looking at him with triumph. "What are you so proud of?" he asked, taking her hand and leading her into his house.

"Just being firm about everything!" she said, then ruined her triumphant moment by tripping and falling into his arms. She gasped with the contact and Ash didn't even move his hand once he realized that it was on her breast.

She straightened up again and took a step backwards. "You are not a gentleman."

Ash laughed softly and looked down at her. "And you're drunk. How about some coffee?" he suggested.

She shook her head. "I'm not drunk and I can't drink coffee this late at night. I'll never get to sleep," she said.

He fixed two cups of coffee anyway and handed her one as she wandered about his home. She didn't even argue with him, just started sipping the coffee as she poked and prodded at the various books on his bookshelf. "Have you read all of these?" she asked, glad that her eyes were actually starting to focus more easily now.

"Yes."

She was impressed. "You're pretty smart then." She turned to grin at him. "But I guess you already proved that, haven't you?"

Ash was sitting in his big leather chair and he'd already turned on the fireplace which was now crackling with the gas logs licking at the top of the firebox. "I kept you out of jail."

She turned to face him, her smile bright and luminous once again. "You did, didn't you?"

"And you left my office when I told you to stay put."

She laughed and nodded her head. "If you want someone to stay put, get a dog."

"But I want you."

"No you don't. You want a dog."

He threw back his head and laughed. "I guarantee that I'm not marrying a dog, Mia. You'll have to get over that and just accept your fate."

She took another sip of the coffee, impressed with how quickly it really was sobering her up. "You'll have to find someone else. I won't marry a man who doesn't trust me."

He sighed and stood up, coming over to loom over her with the fire lighting her features with a soft glow. "Mia, let's get this out in the open and hopefully you'll remember this so we won't ever have this conversation again. I might not have trusted you that first morning, but we were going through a lot of issues then. By the time I took you out to lunch and you wouldn't eat anything because you didn't have your wallet with you, that pretty much clinched it for me."

"What are you talking about?" she demanded, embarrassed by that lunch event all over again.

He pulled her close, taking her coffee cup out of her hand. "A true criminal wouldn't have tried to pay for her own meal. Real criminals do everything they can to get someone else to pay for their lives in one way or another. So from that moment on, I was sure of your innocence."

She pulled back slightly, not sure if she should trust him. She'd done so before and where had that landed her? In a bar drinking margaritas with friends. Not exactly where she'd planned to be tonight.

But at least she wasn't in jail!

"What about all those times you pulled back? All the times you looked at me with horror on your face? As if you'd just done something horrible?"

He pulled her closer, his hands smoothing up her back. "I had done something horrible! You were my client! I was taking advantage of your worried state and that wasn't fair."

She bit her lip. "Was that illegal?" she asked, worried for him now.

He sighed but wouldn't let her move away from him. "Not illegal, but it violated my personal code of ethics and probably all other lawyers' as well."

She cringed. "Okay, so all that backing away after kissing me or touching me, that was just....guilt?"

"Hell yes!"

"So…what does that mean now?"

He lifted her into his arms and carried her back over to where he'd been sitting several minutes ago. "It means that we're getting married now. You love me."

"How do you know that?' she asked, but her arms went around his neck. Could she trust what he was saying?

"Because you gave yourself to me last night. And you said it with the ladies earlier in the evening."

She gasped and pulled back, trying to push against his chest but he wouldn't let her off of his lap. "I did not!" she denied vehemently.

"You did. I have several witnesses. And what's more, I'm in love with you. I probably was in love with you from the moment Autumn told me you saved earthworms," he told her.

She laughed but rolled her eyes. "You're going to have to forget that." Then she hesitated. "Wait a minute, Autumn told you that even before you'd met me. You couldn't have been in love with me then."

He shrugged. "Okay, so maybe love is too strong of a word. But I was fascinated by anyone who would be so worried about a species that has a brain only large enough to survive and can't really experience pain or anxiety over drying out in the hot sun."

She was already shaking her head. "You can't know that. And just put yourself in their position."

He kissed her to stop her argument. And when she was soft and compliant in his arms again, he lifted his head and looked down at her. "I'm still not going to argue about worms," he told her, sliding his hand up her back and causing her to wiggle deliciously.

She grabbed his hand to stop him and refocused on his statement. "So if you were so convinced of my innocence, why did you leave my bed this morning?"

"A combination of my guilt over sleeping with a client, even when I knew I was going to marry said client, and an aching need to protect you, keep you from going back to jail and a sixth sense that something was going to pop up this morning. I knew something was wrong and was racing against the clock."

"Is that why you ignored me in the office? Because you were trying to work?"

"Did I hurt your feelings?" he asked, using his other hand to touch her cheek gently.

"Yes. I thought you were angry with yourself for giving in and making love to me."

"I was furious with myself for violating my code of ethics and determined to fix it so I could still be in your bed tonight without the guilt."

She smiled brightly. "So today was all about making sure I would be in your bed?"

"Exactly. And that you would agree to marry me," he said, moving his head closer to her neck and nuzzling the sensitive skin.

"I haven't said I'll marry you," she contradicted, but she tilted her head, letting her own hand slide up his chest.

"You will," he said and bit her earlobe gently but with enough pressure to make her gasp.

"I might not," she countered.

He slid his hand underneath her sweater. "I have ways of convincing you."

She laughed and grabbed his wrist again. But he wasn't going to allow that. In one swift move, he lifted her up into his arms and carried her over to the sofa where the soft throw blanket was already draped over the back. He pulled it down and set her on top of it, then covered her body with his own. "You're mine, Mia Paulson. And the sooner you accept that, the better because I'm not letting you out of this house until you agree to marry me."

With that threat looming over her, she smiled and snuggled up to his chest. She was more than happy to have him keep her here. Maybe if she refused him over and over again, he would make love to her over and over again. She definitely wouldn't mind that scenario.

"If you insist," she said with a huge grin.

"I love you," he said as he bent to kiss her.

She sighed, wrapping her arms around his neck. "I love you too, you gorgeous man."

Excerpt from "His Unexpected Lover"

"I can't do this," she whispered to herself. "I thought I could, but it's simply too painful."

Kiera's shoulders slumped and she tried to find the answers within the depths of her martini. Unfortunately, the liquid only mocked her, small circles forming on the top and quickly dissipating as if to say, "You never should have come here."

Or maybe the glass was only telling her that a heavy-footed person was walking by.

She held her head up with her forehead, trying to figure out what to do. She'd only been at her new job for a less than a week and already she loved it. The people were fun, hard-working, extremely smart…that all added up to an ideal workplace where she was challenged to excel and stand out, but what was even better, she respected her peers. Instinctively, she knew that The Thorpe Group encouraged competition but, unlike other law firms, didn't condone the backstabbing and win-or-get-out pressure on cases. Oh, they won cases! Clients came to The Thorpe Group for legal advice from all over the country, all over the world even, because they knew that The Thorpe Group would deliver. The difference was that their success was due to a brilliant legal team versus barely ethical legal tactics.

There were other law firms out there with a similar reputation, although none as glamorous as The Thorpe Group. Gaining a few years at this firm on her resume would set her up perfectly for success wherever she wanted to go as a next step.

No, the work and the workers weren't the problem.

Even the location was great. Chicago was a fabulous city with excellent museums, a thriving art community, tons of shopping and a wide range of people with which to interact.

Nope, all of her issues were personal. She'd foolishly convinced herself that she would be able to deal with this problem but, after only a few days, she knew that the issue was bigger than she could handle.

Axel Thorpe.

She'd seen him in the hallway earlier today. And that one sighting, just the glimpse of the man as he walked into a conference room, was why she was here, trying to drown her problem in a martini.

Unfortunately, she realized after ordering that she didn't like martinis.

She also didn't like her body's reaction to seeing Axel Thorpe again. She'd almost embarrassed herself when she'd seen him. She didn't think he'd seen her trip thankfully. Nor had any of her co-workers which was at last something. She'd had to catch herself by grabbing onto a chair which probably looked ridiculous, but at least she hadn't fallen on the floor. She might have passed off the accident as just a fluke, but she'd almost fallen over the conference room table. Not something most people trip over because of its size and obvious placement in the room. But then again, most people hadn't just seen the love of their life after so many years.

Kiera sighed and took another sip of her martini. Maybe she just needed to plow through the drink. Keep forcing it down. Eventually, the alcohol would keep her mind from replaying the scene. She would eventually feel nothing. Maybe that was the way she should handle Axel too. Just keep running into him until her body was numb from the reaction.

Perhaps today's sighting and the humiliating aftermath was just a fluke. Maybe if she just went up and spoke to him, greeted him and asked him how his day was going, she wouldn't be so flustered when she accidentally saw him. Sort of like taking an allergy shot every week to build up one's immune system.

She sighed and took another sip of her martini, her face squinching up ridiculously as she tried to swallow the foul stuff. And she had to acknowledge the stupidity of her idea. Being around him hadn't diminished his appeal or the impact he had on her when she was in college. Every time she'd seen him, she'd been floored. Just like today. Her knees went weak, she had trouble breathing, her whole body started shaking and she was unable to speak coherently.

Maybe it was just an allergy!

She almost giggled to herself and looked down at her drink. Was she reaching the giggle stage after only a few sips of the martini?

She pulled a file folder out of her leather bag, intending to get some work done. She wouldn't think about Axel. She would simply push him from her mind every time he entered. And if she saw him in the hallways at work? Well, she'd known that would happen when she'd accepted the position at The Thorpe Group. The man was one of the co-owners, for goodness sake. She would have been a fool to think she'd never see him.

But after so many years, she'd hoped that she was over him.

She shook her head with derision. Did one ever get over someone like Axel? He really was one in a million. She remembered the first time she'd seen him, laughing in a bar just like this one. She'd been a sophomore at Georgetown University in Washington, D.C. and he'd been clerking for a Supreme Court justice.

He'd been magnificent, she thought with a smile. So tall, so handsome and one could just see the charm and charisma oozing from the man's smile.

Six Years Earlier....

"This place is too crowded," Kiera pointed out, peering through the windows of the upscale bar in Georgetown. "Why don't we go back to our usual hangout?"

Debbie just grabbed Kiera's hand and pulled her deeper into the crowd, obviously eager to be here for some reason. "Because Brian will be there," Debbie replied, referring to her ex-boyfriend, almost yelling over the noise of the bar. "And I really don't want to run into him again. He's still angry about our breakup last week."

She quickly shifted out of the way of someone who almost spilled beer on her. "This place is a bit rowdier than the places we usually hang out," Kiera cautioned.

Debbie looked around and smiled. "It's nice! I like trying out new places and meeting new people."

Except that Debbie had invited all of their old friends here so they probably wouldn't meet anyone they didn't already know. "I'm not sure I'm all that adventurous tonight, Debbie," Kiera cautioned. It wasn't so much that she wasn't into trying new things, but she preferred less crowded conditions than this place that had wall to wall people.

"Just pretend for one night," Debbie laughed back, pulling Kiera up to the bar and ordered two beers.

Kiera shook her head but followed her friend, not sure this was such a good idea. "Fine," she agreed and tried to hide the weird feeling that had come over her suddenly. Midterms had just finished and she had a bit of breathing room before her next paper was due so it wouldn't be a bad thing to relax for a few hours. "But we're not staying late." Was she being too cautious? Probably, she told herself as she slipped between a couple that was heavy into a debate on the latest political wranglings. It was hard to avoid those kinds of discussions in a Georgetown bar. Not only were they mere miles from the heart of the federal buildings, the area was teeming with history. The streets were mostly cobblestones from the colonial period and even a small townhouse would cost well over one million dollars. The cobblestones were ballast from the rum trade but the political debates were due to the proximity to the federal government. She suspected that many of the people here were either international studies students, political science majors or were interning for a senator or representative.

"This is awesome," Debbie called back to her, grinning from ear to ear, obviously excited to be in a new setting instead of their normal haunts. The bar was darker, probably proud of the bare bricks and heavy, wooden beams overhead that might or might not date back to the colonial period. If they weren't, Kiera doubted the owner would 'fess up to having new beams. Many of the establishments promoted the "old time" feel of their buildings by refurbishing so that the décor was reminiscent of colonial times, but with all the bells and whistles of modern conveniences. Of course, there was the one trendy bar she knew of that bragged about having bullet holes in the walls. Not that they claimed the bullets were colonial, but every bar had to have its quirks, she supposed.

She took the beer Debbie handed her and then turned around, trying to find a place to sit down. The odds of finding a chair or stool in a place this crowded would be pretty slim, she thought while her eyes surveyed the room.

Kiera noticed him the moment Debbie's back was turned. He was in a group of four or five other men, all of them laughing about something. But not him. He was staring right back at her. His eyes seemed to capture hers but that look was so powerful, his gaze so strong that it jolted her all the way down to her toes. More than just her eyes were captured. Her whole body was frozen in place, the noise and crowds, the damp smell of beer and other drinks…all of it just disappeared from her consciousness as she stared right back at him. She couldn't breathe and she couldn't pull her eyes away, she couldn't even move.

She hadn't even realized that Debbie had turned around and was trying engage her in conversation until Debbie breathed, "Who is that?"

Kiera struggled, but she was finally able to pull her eyes away and glanced at her friend. To her horror, Debbie was staring at the man! Her man! And there was a great deal of interest on Debbie's lovely features. Jealousy, hot and powerful stabbed through Kiera's body. She didn't like her friend even looking at a man she already considered to be hers.

Okay, so that was ridiculous. She couldn't claim a human being simply because they were looking at each other from across the room. But there was no way to suppress the furious feelings that surged through Kiera as her friend surveyed the tall, handsome stranger. Kiera tried to be rational about this. She had no claim on the man. But regardless, Kiera was suddenly incensed that Debbie had dared to look at the guy. It was a sudden and all-consuming jealousy, something Kiera had never experienced before so she wasn't sure how to handle that level of intensity. Men had never affected her in the past. To her, they were simply other human beings she could study with or joke with during non-study hours.

It was completely different with this man. And completely irrational.

Instead of revealing her jealousy, Kiera took a sip of her beer and pulled Debbie through the crowd until they couldn't see the man anymore, although Debbie's blond head kept craning at different angles to try and take another gander at the man.

Debbie wasn't shy about letting a guy know she was interested. But didn't she need a bit of time to get over Brian? Debbie had just broken up with her boyfriend earlier this week! What was she doing ogling another man so quickly? It was ridiculous and disrespectful of Brian's feelings not to mention the three years they'd been together.

Kiera tried hard to ignore her jealousy, pushing Debbie to talk about classes and their friends in an effort to distract her from the gorgeous man. When a couple more friends showed up, Kiera was relieved to finally have support distracting Debbie from the man Kiera had already claimed, at least mentally. Not that she would do anything about her gnawing desire to find out more about the tall, intensely handsome man with the piercing, ice blue eyes.

Kiera wasn't like Debbie. Where Kiera was shy and introverted, Debbie was the party girl, the one that pushed Kiera to get out and have more fun. Debbie also didn't hide her interest in the opposite sex. When Debbie wanted a man, she walked right up to him and started talking to him. Kiera hadn't ever felt this way, but she knew that she wouldn't go up to that man tonight. She wasn't that brave. Besides, she'd never felt that way about a man before. And he hadn't even touched her! No, she couldn't handle him so it was better to just stay away from that kind of...whatever it was.

An hour later, Kiera desperately needed to use the ladies' room. Unfortunately, the man she'd spotted earlier had been positioned right next to the hallway where the bathrooms were located. She wiggled in her chair, determined to ignore the need. But when Debbie popped up with the same intention, Kiera wasn't going to allow her to go alone. "I'll come with you," she said, determined to keep Debbie and the stranger from seeing each other again. Kiera knew she couldn't have the man. She wasn't glamorous or rich or any of those adjectives that would apply to the woman on that kind of man's arm. She was passably pretty with curly brown hair that tended to get out of control. She had a good enough figure but she wasn't any lingerie model.

In short, Kiera knew she was just an average kind of gal.

Debbie, on the other hand, was not only blond and beautiful, she had a way about her that seemed to draw men into her realm. She was fun and nice not to mention extremely intelligent. And over the past year, they'd been good friends and study partners. But at this moment, Kiera could honestly say that she hated Debbie. Because Kiera knew that Debbie was going to talk to the stranger. Kiera could see it in Debbie's eyes and was helpless to stop the action. Kiera felt helpless, desperate to keep Debbie from acquiring yet another conquest, but unable to come up with any ideas on how to stop her from working her magic.

Kiera had no doubt that Debbie was going to approach the man. It was in her eyes and Kiera glanced over at the man, her eyes worried as she gauged the distance between Debbie and the man.

But as soon as she found him through the crowd, she realized that he was looking at her!

Debbie was even primping, doing her best to get noticed. Kiera looked from Debbie to the stranger, wondering when he would notice the blond beauty standing next to her.

The stranger's eyes never wavered and Kiera's stomach did flip flops at the realization.

They made their way down the hallway to the ladies' room and Kiera breathed a sigh of relief. One gauntlet down, one more to go. Maybe she could get Debbie out of the bar. Maybe if they just left, Debbie wouldn't have time to set her sights on…

"Did you see him again?" Debbie gushed as they both washed their hands.

Kiera's throat constricted when she noticed the light of intent in Debbie's eyes. "I'm going to talk to him," she declared. Kiera sighed with resignation. When Debbie went on the prowl, men tended to fall to their knees and worship her.

She fluffed her blond hair one more time and Kiera wished she had done something more interesting with her out-of-control curls. They floated around her like some sort of bohemian gypsy instead of being smooth and glossy-straight like Debbie's blond hair. Debbie even had those pretty blue eyes that she could bat at any man and have him fall at her feet, desperate to do her bidding. Kiera stared at her boring brown eyes, wishing for the first time that her face could be more interesting, more devastatingly beautiful. Her lashes might be long, but her mouth was too wide and too full, her nose too small to be anything other than cute instead of sophisticated and interesting. Her cheeks weren't gaunt and she even had a sprinkling of freckles over the bridge of her nose and her cheeks that she normally covered up with makeup but hadn't bothered tonight, much to her irritation now.

With a sigh, Kiera looked behind her at Debbie's luscious figure, wondering how long it would be before Debbie had the stranger wrapped around her pinky finger.

They stepped out of the hallway, Kiera holding her head down, not wanting to watch Debbie snag yet another man. Why couldn't her friend leave this one alone? Why couldn't she just let one, this special one, go about his business and not make him fall under her spell?

Suddenly, her path was blocked and someone was holding a beer towards her. She looked up, but all she saw was a denim clad chest. It was an extraordinarily muscular chest, she noticed. Her heartbeat picked up rapidly because she knew exactly who this man was. Her eyes continued to climb and she couldn't believe it when her light brown eyes captured the ice blue ones of her stranger.

The man was smiling down at her, not even noticing her blond friend beside her. Of course, Kiera had no idea if Debbie was still there or if she'd moved on. It was just this man and herself and her racing heart.

"I wish I could come up with some witty line to get your attention, but I'll admit, I'm stumped," he said.

Kiera tried to smile. She tried to catch her breath. But with this man standing so close to her, his body heat and that incredible male scent wafting towards her, she just couldn't think. "I believe I'm in the same situation," she replied nervously.

He looked down at her hands and smiled. "I noticed you were drinking beers. I got you another one," he said, referring to the second beer he still had in his hands. "I know that was forward of me, but..."

Kiera straightened quickly, not wanting him to think she was rejecting the offer. "No, that's very kind of you," she said, taking the beer. But her hand accidentally touched his and she felt some sort of...spark? She pulled back quickly, unsure of what was going on. Unfortunately, at the same time, he was releasing the beer. The result was both of them grabbing for the beer again, fumbling and beer spilled out, landing on her hand.

"I'm so sorry!" she gasped, horrified at how clumsy she was acting.

"My fault," his deep, sexy voice replied.

"No, really, I was the clumsy one," she countered, looking up into those blue eyes once again. And she couldn't move. Not even to take a breath. They looked into each other's eyes and it was as if the noise of the bar once again faded away leaving only the noise of her heartbeat. There was only this large man standing in front of her and the cold beer in her hand.

"I'm Axel Thorpe," he said softly, that deep baritone soothing over her skin like a balm.

"I'm Kiera Ward," she replied. As his large, strong hand took hers, she prayed hard that her knees wouldn't give out on her and she wouldn't throw up because she was suddenly feeling like something had just exploded inside of her stomach.

COMMENTS FROM THE AUTHOR

For some fun visuals on Ash and Mia, go to:

http://www.pinterest.com/elennoxromances/his-captive-lover-mia-and-ash/

If you have time, please take a moment to write a review on whichever platform you purchased this book. It not only helps guide others who might purchase this book, but I also love hearing from my readers – the good, the bad and the ugly. Some readers tell me there's too much sex, some tell me I should add more, others criticize my grammar and others tell me they love my books. Everything you write, I use to improve my next story. If you love what I write, let me know because I'll continue writing in the same way. If you think I should improve in some way, please let me know. I have a very tough skin and can take it – although I absolutely LOVE the positive reviews/comments.

If you would like to contact me directly, I can be reached at elizabeth@elizabethlennox.com. I try very hard to answer all e-mails because I love hearing from readers so much! It is a thrill to hear from you. But I apologize in advance if I miss responding to your message. Sometimes, things get lost in the inbox. I'm one of those non-techy people so I don't always see things that others might think are obvious. It isn't a slight – I promise. It is just that my mind is off in romance-world and not in the techy-world (much more fun/interesting/exciting in my romance-world even though my husband bangs his head against the desk sometimes when I don't understand the techy-world).

BOOKS BY ELIZABETH LENNOX

The Texas Tycoon's Temptation

The Royal Cordova Trilogy
Escaping a Royal Wedding
The Man's Outrageous Demands
Mistress To The Prince

The Attracelli Family Series
Never Dare A Tycoon
Falling For The Boss
Risky Negotiations
Proposal To Love
Love's Not Terrifying
Romantic Acquisition

The Billionaire's Terms: Prison Or Passion
The Sheik's Love Child
The Sheik's Unfinished Business
The Greek Tycoon's Lover
The Sheik's Sensuous Trap
The Greek's Baby Bargain
The Italian's Bedroom Deal
The Billionaire's Gamble
The Tycoon's Seduction Plan
The Sheik's Rebellious Mistress
The Sheik's Missing Bride
Blackmailed By The Billionaire
The Billionaire's Runaway Bride
The Billionaire's Elusive Lover
The Intimate, Intricate Rescue
The Sisterhood Trilogy
The Sheik's Virgin Lover
The Billionaire's Impulsive Lover
The Russian's Tender Lover
The Billionaire's Gentle Rescue

The Tycoon's Toddler Surprise

The Tycoon's Tender Triumph
The Sheik's Mysterious Mistress
The Duke's Willful Wife
The Sheik's Secret Twins
The Tycoon's Marriage Exchange
The Russian's Furious Fiancee
The Tycoon's Misunderstood Bride

Love By Accident Series
The Sheik's Pregnant Lover
The Sheik's Furious Bride
The Duke's Runaway Princess

The Russian's Pregnant Mistress

The Lovers Exchange Series
The Earl's Outrageous Lover
The Tycoon's Resistant Lover

The Sheik's Reluctant Lover
The Spanish Tycoon's Temptress

The Berutelli Escape Series
Resisting The Tycoon's Seduction
The Billionaire's Secretive Enchantress

The Big Apple Brotherhood
The Billionaire's Pregnant Lover
The Sheik's Rediscovered Lover
The Tycoon's Defiant Southern Belle

The Sheik's Dangerous Lover (free novella)

The Thorpe Brothers Series
His Captive Lover
His Unexpected Lover
His Secretive Lover
His Challenging Lover

The Sheik's Defiant Fiancée (Free Novella)

The Prince's Resistant Lover (Free Novella)
The Tycoon's Make Believe Fiancee (Free Novella)

The Friendship Series
The Billionaires Masquerade
The Russian's Dangerous Game
The Sheik's Beautiful Intruder

The Love and Danger Series – Romantic Mysteries
Intimate Desires
Intimate Caresses
Intimate Secrets – July 2014
Intimate Whispers – August 2014

www.ingramcontent.com/pod-product-compliance
Lightning Source LLC
Chambersburg PA
CBHW070458130626
46555CB00003B/1063